Punishment

Punishment

Ferdinand von Schirach

Translated from the German by Katharina Hall

BASKERVILLE
An imprint of JOHN MURRAY

First published as *Strafe* in Germany in 2018
by Luchterhand Literaturverlag
First published in Great Britain in 2021 by
Baskerville, an imprint of John Murray
An Hachette UK company

1

A CIP catalogue record for this title is
available from the British Library

Hardback ISBN 978-1-529-34568-1
eBook ISBN 978-1-529-34570-4

Typeset in Sabon by Hewer Text UK Ltd, Edinburgh
Printed and bound in Great Britain by Clays Ltd, Elcograf S.p.A.

John Murray policy is to use papers that are natural, renewable
and recyclable products and made from wood grown in sustainable
forests. The logging and manufacturing processes are expected to
conform to the environmental regulations of the country of origin.

Baskerville, an imprint of John Murray
Carmelite House
50 Victoria Embankment
London EC4Y 0DZ

www.johnmurraypress.co.uk

Contents

Most happens when all is still.

Søren Kierkegaard

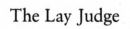

The Lay Judge

Katharina was raised in the Upper Black Forest. Eleven farms at an altitude of 1,100 metres, with a chapel and a grocery that opened only on Mondays. They lived in the last building along, a three-storey farmhouse with a low-lying roof. It was her mother's family home. Beyond the farmhouse lay the forest; beyond the forest lay the rocks; beyond the rocks lay yet more forest. She was the only child in the village.

Her father was the deputy director of a paper mill, her mother a teacher. Both worked down in the city. At the age of eleven, Katharina often spent time at her father's workplace after school. She sat in the office as he negotiated prices, discounts and delivery dates. She listened as he made phone calls and explained everything to her so that she understood. In the school holidays, he took her on business trips. She packed his bags, laid out his suits, and waited at the hotel for him to return from meetings. At thirteen, she was half a head taller than him; slender, with a fair complexion and hair that was almost black. Her father called her Snow White, and laughed when someone told him he had a very young wife.

Two weeks after Katharina's fourteenth birthday, the first snow of the year fell. It was very bright and very cold. New wood shingles lay stacked in front of the house; her father was planning to mend the roof before the onset of winter. As usual, her mother drove her to school. There was a truck up ahead of them. Her mother hadn't spoken all morning.

'Your father's fallen in love with someone else,' she said now. There was snow on the trees and snow on the rocks. They overtook the truck, which had TROPICAL FRUIT written along its side, each letter a different colour. 'With his secretary,' said her mother. She was driving too fast. Katharina knew the secretary; she had always been friendly. All she could think was that her father hadn't said anything to her. She dug her nails into her school bag until it hurt.

Her father moved to a house in the city. Katharina didn't see him after that.

Six months later, the windows of the farmhouse were boarded up, the pipes drained and the electricity turned off. Katharina and her mother moved to Bonn, where they had relatives.

It took Katharina a year to stop speaking in dialect. She wrote political essays for the school newspaper. When she was sixteen, a local newspaper printed one of her pieces for the first time. She scrutinised everything that she did.

Because she got top marks in her final school exams, she had to give the graduation speech in assembly. It was an uncomfortable experience. Later, at the party, she had too much to drink. She danced with a boy from her class. She kissed him and felt his erection through his jeans. He wore imitation horn-rimmed glasses and had damp hands. She sometimes thought about other men – self-confident, mature men who turned their heads to look at her and told her she was pretty. But they stayed beyond her reach, too far from what she knew.

The young man drove her home. She masturbated him in the car outside her house while she thought about the mistakes she had made when giving her speech. Then she went upstairs. In the bathroom, she used some nail scissors to cut her wrist again. It bled more than usual. When she tried to find a dressing, little bottles and tubes fell into the sink. 'I'm damaged goods,' she thought.

After leaving school, she moved into a two-room apartment with a school friend and began to study Political Science. After a couple of semesters she got a job as a teaching assistant. At weekends she worked as an underwear model for department store catalogues.

In her fourth semester, she interned for a member of the State Parliament. He came from the Eifel region; his parents had a fashion business there. It was his first term in office. He looked like an older version of her earlier friends: still completely self-absorbed, more boy than man, he was short and stocky with a round, amiable face. She didn't think he was cut out for politics, but kept that to herself. On a tour of his constituency, he introduced her to his friends. *He's proud of me*, she thought. At dinner, after discussing his schedule for the following day, he leaned over the table and kissed her. They went back to his hotel room. He was so aroused that he came straight away. She did her best to soothe his embarrassment.

She held on to her apartment, but almost always stayed at his place. Sometimes they went away, but only for short breaks as he was very busy. She was tactful when correcting his speeches; she didn't want to hurt his feelings. When they slept together, he lost control of his body. She found that moving.

She didn't celebrate her exam results; she told her friends and family she was too tired. She was already in bed when her boyfriend arrived home late after an event. He was wearing the tie she had given him. He opened a bottle of champagne that he had brought back and asked her to marry him. He stood by the edge of the bed. She didn't have to give an answer right away, he said with a glass in his hand.

That night she went into the bathroom, sat on the floor of the shower, and let the hot water run over her until her skin was practically scalded. *It'll always be there*, she thought. She had been aware of it even at school – she'd called it background radiation then, like the microwaves found throughout the universe. She cried silently, then the worst of it passed and she felt ashamed.

'We should visit my parents next week,' he said at breakfast.

'I'm not coming,' she said.

Then she talked about his freedom and about her freedom, and about everything they still wanted to do. She talked at length about all those things, which were neither true nor relevant to their situation. The heat of the midsummer day came through the open windows. She no longer knew what was right or what was wrong, and at a certain point there was nothing more to say. She rose, and cleared the table that he had laid. She felt wounded and empty and very tired.

She got back into bed. When she heard him crying in the next room, she got up again and went to him. They slept together one last time, in a way that suggested it meant something, but it no longer meant anything and wasn't a commitment.

That afternoon she packed her things into two plastic bags. She put the key to his apartment on the table.

'I'm not the person I want to be,' she said. He didn't look at her.

She walked past the university, then over the scorched grass of the *Hofgarten* and up the tree-lined avenue to the palace. She sat on a bench and drew up her legs. Her shoes were covered in dust. The sphere on the palace roof shone oxide green. The wind turned to the east, grew stronger, and it started to rain.

Her apartment was muggy. She undressed, lay on the bed and fell instantly asleep. When she woke up, she heard the rain and the wind and the bells of the nearby church. Then she fell asleep again, and when she awoke a second time it was very quiet.

She started working for a political foundation. Her job was to look after delegates during conferences – politicians, businessmen, lobbyists. The hotels smelled of liquid soap; at breakfast, the men flipped their ties over their shoulders so they wouldn't get stained. Later, she had only vague memories of this period.

Gradually, things improved. The chairman of the foundation recognised her abilities: people liked her and, because she was very reserved, said more than they intended. The chairman made her his advisor. She accompanied him, wrote press releases, counselled him, suggested strategies. The chairman said that she was very good, but she thought she was worthless, a kind of imposter, her work insignificant. They sometimes slept together when they were on trips; it seemed to go with the territory.

After three years of living like this, her body began to ache. She kept losing weight. When she had time off, she was too exhausted to meet up with anyone.

Every appointment, every phone call, every email felt too much for her. Her mobile lay by her bed at night.

In a gap between two conferences, she needed to have a wisdom tooth extracted. She broke down at the dental surgery, and because she couldn't stop crying, the dentist injected her with a sedative. It had too strong an effect: she lost consciousness and only came round once she was in hospital.

She sat up. She was wearing just a hospital gown, which was open at the back. A yellow curtain was drawn across the window. Later, a psychologist came to see her. He was calm and gentle. She talked with him for a long time. He said that she reacted too strongly to others; she needed to take care of herself and to understand that she was her own person. Things would end badly if she kept going the same way.

A week later, she handed in her resignation at the foundation.

Four months after her breakdown, the chairman called her. He asked whether she was feeling better. A company in Berlin was looking for a press spokeswoman, and he had recommended her. Young people, a software company. Perhaps she'd be interested; either way, he wished her all the best.

She knew that she needed to work again; her days had long since lost their rhythm. She got in touch with the company and flew to Berlin a week later. She had often visited the city, but only really knew the government quarter, and the inside of conference rooms and air-conditioned bars.

The head of the company was younger than her, with very white teeth and light blue eyes. He showed her the app they had developed. He gave her a tour of the office; the staff were also very young, most of them staring at their screens.

That evening at the hotel, she pushed an armchair in front of the open window, took off her shoes, and put her feet up on the windowsill. The trees in front of the building were glowing alternately green and red from the nearby traffic lights. In an apartment across the street, someone put the lights on; she saw bookshelves and pictures, and a blue and white vase on a windowsill framed by curtains. The room smelled of the lime and chestnut trees beyond the window, and of the exhaust fumes from the taxis waiting by the entrance downstairs.

She flew back the following morning. She thought of her first boyfriend and the trip they had taken to Provence, then along the coast and across the Pyrenees to Spain. It had been their first big holiday: a slow train, stopping every half an hour at stations where no one got on or off. Rose and lavender fields right by the railway line, the countryside welcoming and bright. She had laid her head in her boyfriend's lap. She couldn't see the sea, but could sense exactly where it was.

When the plane landed, she stayed in her seat for too long. Someone told her that she needed to disembark and she nodded. She was freezing as she made her way through the arrivals hall. She got into a taxi. There were photos stuck on the dashboard: a woman wearing a headscarf, a boy in a football shirt. The car drove over a bridge, the Rhine flowing wide in the sunshine.

Katharina began working for the software company in Berlin. The job was easy: press releases, interviews, the occasional dinner with clients. She was the only woman in the office. Once she saw a picture of herself on one of the computer screens. Someone had photoshopped her head onto a naked woman's body. Every now and then a programmer would try to flirt with her. She didn't go out much; she preferred to be on her own.

*   *   *

The letter from the regional court was printed on recycled paper. It informed her that she had been appointed a lay judge for a term of five years. She phoned the number on the letterhead and said there must be a misunderstanding; she didn't have time to take this on. The man at the other end sounded bored. He told her that she could apply to be excused. He sounded like he'd said this hundreds of times before. She could decline the role if she was a member of the State Parliament, the Bundestag, the Bundesrat or the European Parliament. Or if she was a doctor or a nurse. It was all in the Courts Constitution Act, she should take a look for herself. If she still thought she had grounds to be excused, she could put it in writing, and the court would decide the matter in conjunction with the public prosecutor's office.

Katharina consulted the software company's lawyer. He told her that she didn't stand a chance.

On the morning of her first trial she arrived early at the court. Her ID was checked. It took her a while to find the right room. A court officer read her summons, nodded, unlocked a conference room next to the courtroom and asked her to wait there. She sat down at the table. The judge arrived sometime later. They discussed the weather and her work. The judge told her that they would be hearing a domestic abuse case that day. The second lay judge turned up just before the trial was due to begin. He was a teacher at a training college. This was his fifth one already, he said.

At a few minutes past nine they entered the courtroom through a side door. Everybody rose. The judge declared the session open, but said that a lay judge would be sworn in first.

Then he read the oath aloud, sentence by sentence. Katharina had to repeat it while raising her right hand; before her lay a piece of paper with the sentences printed on it in a large font. After that, everyone sat down. The accused was seated next to his defence counsel; a court officer was reading a newspaper. There were no members of the public present.

The judge welcomed the defence counsel and the public prosecutor. He asked the accused for his date of birth and his address. The man had been on remand for four months. The clerk noted everything down. She was sitting next to Katharina. Her handwriting was illegible.

The public prosecutor stood up and read out the charges. The man had *wounded his wife's body with intent*. The defence counsel said that his client did not wish to make a statement at this time. The judge asked the court officer to call the witness.

The witness took a seat and placed her handbag on the floor. The judge told her that she wasn't obliged to say anything as she was the wife of the accused, but that if she chose to do so, it must be the truth.

It all had to do with the yellow notes, said the woman. Her husband wrote her notes, he'd been doing it for years. He always had a block in his pocket, those sticky yellow bits of paper. On the notes he wrote what she should do while he was at work. He stuck the notes on the dirty dishes (*Wash up*), on the laundry (*Clean*), or on the fridge (*Cheese*, or whatever else she was supposed to buy). He stuck the notes everywhere. After a while, she couldn't take it anymore. She told him that she couldn't stand seeing those yellow bits of paper – after all, she knew what she needed to do. But he hadn't stopped; he'd kept on sticking the notes. He'd said that he, the one who was out working all day, had to look after the housework as well. 'Thick as two short planks' had been his favourite expression for her. She was no good, he told her daily. She was no good.

He used to accuse her of being unable to have children. That had hurt for a number of years. But she'd got used to it, and now he didn't say it anymore.

In the summer, they were almost always outside – down at the allotments between the motorway and the airport. They had a little shed there. He'd say it was even down to him to look after the garden. Just once, she had bought some blue flowers herself at the garden centre and planted them there. He had dug them up again. They didn't go, he'd said.

The judge leafed through the case file. The husband already had four convictions for assaulting her; the hospital had contacted the police each time. On the most recent occasion, he had hit her with the oar of a dinghy and been given a suspended sentence. That was why he had been held on remand this time, and if he were found guilty could have his suspended sentence revoked.

'The thing is, he's not himself when he drinks,' said the woman. He was a good man, but drinking had ruined him.

On the day in question, they'd set up the barbecue in the garden. The neighbours were there as well. She had put the sausages on the grill. Her husband had sat with the neighbours at the table outside. They'd been talking and drinking beer. She'd gone into the kitchen to get some bread. Then she'd walked back out to the grill. It had been 'really odd'. She heard her husband talking, and suddenly she couldn't have cared less about the sausages. She watched as they burst open, as the fat dripped onto the coals and the meat charred. Her husband had come over and yelled that she was too stupid even to barbecue, and had hit her on the back of the head with his hand. She didn't care, she hardly noticed, she simply didn't care about anything. Then he'd kicked over the barbecue. The coals had spilled out and burned her leg and foot. Their neighbours had driven her to hospital; her husband hadn't gone with them. She only had small scars. 'Nothing serious,' she said.

The judge read out the hospital's initial report. Yes, that was all correct, said the woman. The judge asked Katharina and the other lay judge whether they had any questions for the woman. The other lay judge shook his head. Katharina was pale; she was worried that her voice might fail her.

'What were you thinking about when you stopped caring?' she asked.

The woman raised her head and looked at her. She needed a moment.

'About our car,' she said. It had been their first car, back when they were still young and had been married for just six months. They'd bought it second-hand from a dealer. It had been much too expensive for them and they had taken out a loan. A light blue VW Beetle with a sunroof and chrome bumpers. On the first day, they had washed and vacuumed and polished it together at the petrol station. Then they had gone to bed, and the following morning they had stood side by side at the apartment window and looked down at the car, which was gleaming on the street in the sun. He had put his arm around her shoulders. That's what she had been thinking about. She had wanted to make everything nice for him, she said, a nice life. She had wanted to be there for him.

Katharina looked at the woman, and the woman looked at Katharina. Katharina began to cry. She cried because the witness's story was her story, and because she understood the woman's life, and because there was loneliness in all things. No one spoke.

The lawyer stood up. He needed to make an *urgent application*, he said quietly. The judge nodded. He announced that there would be an hour's break in the proceedings.

In the conference room, the judge said that the defence wanted to veto Katharina due to *concerns about bias*. If the application were successful, the trial would collapse because there was no substitute lay judge. The judge sat down; he looked very tired now.

Could she apologise, asked Katharina? She was so sorry.

'That won't make any difference,' said the judge. 'Go and have a coffee and compose yourself.' Katharina and the other lay judge went to the court canteen. These things happen, he said, she shouldn't reproach herself. Someone was piling plates and cups onto a trolley. 'I can't stay here,' said Katharina. They walked down the stairs and through the corridors and then out onto the street.

When the trial resumed, the lawyer stood up and read out his application. A judge was allowed to have feelings and to show them, he said. The law wanted people to judge cases, not machines. But the vetoed lay judge had reacted far too strongly. To an unbiased third-party observer, she no longer appeared neutral, detached or impartial. It was a complex application; the lawyer quoted a number of court rulings. Over and over again, he called Katharina '*the vetoed lay judge*'.

Katharina had to write an *official statement* in the conference room, just three or four sentences long. She should state in her own words whether or not she was biased, said the judge. It had to be the truth. The sunlight fell through the tall windows. The other lay judge drank coffee from a plastic cup.

It was true what the lawyer had said about her, Katharina wrote. She was biased.

The defendant's custody order was revoked and he was released. Four months later he smashed in his wife's head with a hammer; she died on the way to the hospital. There was a picture of her in the newspaper.

Katharina wrote a long letter to the Federal Ministry of Justice. She asked to be removed from the list of lay judges and to be dismissed from her honorary position.

The court rejected her application.

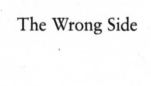

The Wrong Side

It wasn't far from the S-Bahn station to the lake where they planned to spend the day. At first, they could only hear the flies. 'Stop,' he said, and gripped her hand. The man was lying on his front. No one screamed and nothing changed. The heat was the same, the luminous grasses and the breeze. But individual details came sharply into focus: the dead man's black, sticky hair, and the flies, which were blue-green and moving very quickly.

~

Schlesinger had once been a good lawyer. 'Criminal defence,' he'd liked to say, 'is a David and Goliath battle.' He had always believed he stood on the right side.

For a long time, everything had gone well. He had set up a successful legal practice and landed increasingly bigger cases. Then he defended a man accused of abusing his children. He was acquitted: there was insufficient evidence to convict. The man drove home, shoved his two-year-old son into the washing machine and turned it on.

Schlesinger began to drink. But because he was very experienced, and knew the judges and public prosecutors, it took a while for anyone to notice. He downed herbal schnapps miniatures in the toilets during court breaks. He lied to his clients, said that he could get them off, promised acquittals and lenient sentences. They believed him and handed over their money, because he'd once had a good reputation and they wanted to believe anyone who promised them freedom. Schlesinger stopped keeping a record of his earnings and paid hardly any taxes. If the trials went wrong and the sentences were too high, he accused his clients of bringing it on themselves because they'd kept something from him. He got away with it for a while. But there came a point when no one fell for it anymore, because he'd lost too many trials and smelled of alcohol in the mornings.

Schlesinger's wife had hung on for a long time. When she finally told him to move out, he could understand why. The two children stayed with her. Even when she filed for divorce, he didn't blame anyone else for his failure as a husband. That was something he had never done.

He made a living from small cases – neighbourhood disputes, pub brawls and drug offences. His clients were street dealers who swallowed the little bags of heroin they had stashed in their mouths when the police came after them. His evenings were spent in a grubby Chinese restaurant. He sat in the back room and played cards there almost every night. He had defended gambling addicts in the past: nervous, hypersensitive people who didn't want to grow up. Now he understood why they only felt safe at the gaming table. Here, the rules were simple and clear, and as long as the game was running, there was nothing else in the world but that room and the cards.

The Chinese always had one or two professional players at the table. Schlesinger knew he stood no chance of winning. Later, when he was very lucid or very drunk, he realised that he was like all the other addicts: he wanted to lose.

Schlesinger had once been good-looking and women had found him attractive, but now he was fifteen kilos underweight and his suits hung off him. He slept on the sofa at his chambers and showered in a tiny bathroom behind the kitchenette. He let his secretary go. He had long since viewed himself as a ruin of a man.

Schlesinger was still on the list of defence lawyers circulated to examining judges. Every three months he was on standby duty, and had to be available in case someone was arrested and needed a legal aid lawyer. Most of the time his mobile didn't ring, and if it did, it was for insignificant cases that brought in no money. But that night was different. The judge who phoned said it was a murder case. The suspect was accused of shooting her husband. Two days ago, he, the judge, had issued a warrant for her to be held in custody on a charge of murder. The suspect had been detained yesterday evening and would be coming before him in an hour. She needed a court-appointed defence counsel. Schlesinger said that he was on his way, and ended the call.

He looked at his watch. It was half past one in the morning. He had fallen asleep in his clothes, his shirt was covered in cigarette ash, empty bottles lay on the floor. He went into the bathroom and took a cold shower. He found some trousers in the piles of clothes on the floor and pulled on a roll-neck jumper as he couldn't find a clean shirt. In the McDonald's two doors down from his chambers, he bought a takeaway coffee, then hailed a taxi that took him to the Criminal Court in Turmstraße.

Schlesinger had known the judge for twenty years. They reminisced about past cases while they were waiting. The judge complained, as he did every time, about how the police always brought him suspects in the middle of the night.

'Go and see the woman now, Dr Schlesinger,' said the judge. 'Then we can get it over and done with. It looks to me like a hopeless case. Take the warrant with you and talk to her.'

The duty officer accompanied Schlesinger through the low door and down the steep, narrow stairs. There was a vast labyrinth of poorly lit corridors beneath the building, which connected the prison to the courtrooms. Everyone working there called them 'the catacombs'. A female officer unlocked one of the holding cells. The air was stuffy; it smelled of sweat, food, and stale cigarette smoke. Prisoners had scribbled obscene drawings and sentences in numerous languages on the walls. Schlesinger was familiar with the room and the situation – he had been through it all hundreds of times before.

He introduced himself to the woman and sat down. He knew from the warrant that she was forty-three years old. Her eyes were a light green, and she was wearing a beige dress with black shoes.

'I didn't kill my husband.' She said it as if she were remarking on the weather.

'OK, but unfortunately that's not the main issue,' said Schlesinger. 'The question is whether the public prosecutor's office has enough evidence to convince the court that you did.'

'Will I be able to go home later?' she asked.

She doesn't belong here, thought Schlesinger, *but then again, who does?*

'I'm afraid not. The judge received the case files the day before yesterday and issued a warrant to have you taken into custody. That's why you've been detained. In a moment, we'll be called to the judge's chambers. He'll read you the warrant and ask if you have anything to say. If you can't disprove the charge immediately, you'll be held on remand until the trial.'

'What should I say?'

'Nothing for now. We don't know the findings of the investigation yet. As soon as I get access to the case files, I'll visit you in the detention centre. We'll take a look at everything and see what we can do. Right now, anything you say is a risk. Did you make a statement to the police?'

'Yes, I've told the police everything I know. I'm innocent.' The woman looked at Schlesinger. Then comprehension dawned. 'I guess everyone says that.'

'Yes, everyone says that. And it won't impress anyone here.'

They carried on talking until the officer entered the cell and said that it was time.

The judge asked the woman to confirm her name, then read out the warrant and summarised the investigative findings for the accused. He spoke in a rapid monotone. 'Your husband's body was found by two young people at the lake,' he said. 'He was killed by a shot to the back of the head. A pistol lay next to the body. Whether the projectile in your husband's head originated from this gun has yet to be established, but according to a preliminary assessment by firearms experts, it's likely. The pistol is yours, as you yourself have told the police. You claim that you inherited it from your father. The gun, the cartridges in the weapon's magazine, and the cartridge case found lying in the grass had your fingerprints on them. The investigators questioned your neighbours. They all said that you and your husband argued a lot. The arguments were sometimes so loud that the neighbours complained to the landlord about the noise. Two weeks before his death, your husband took out a life insurance policy worth 800,000 euros, naming you as the beneficiary. You have no verifiable alibi for the presumed time of death. You claim that you were at home by yourself – at least that's what you told the police.'

The judge paused. He closed the file and looked straight at the accused.

'Let me sum up as follows: you had a motive, an opportunity and a weapon. And you have no alibi. You're not obliged to respond to the accusations now, but you may make a further statement if you wish and apply for additional evidence to be heard. I imagine you've already discussed this with your defence lawyer. How do you wish to proceed?'

'My client does not wish to comment,' said Schlesinger.

'That's fine. In that case, the warrant is upheld,' said the judge.

'I apply for my client be released from custody,' said Schlesinger. 'She has no previous convictions and has lived here for half her life. She has an apartment in Berlin and has worked as a buyer for a fashion company for twelve years. We could set bail, confiscate her passport—'

'No, Counsel for the Defence,' interrupted the judge. 'If I remember your client's police statement correctly, she has a wealth of foreign contacts. Her parents live in America and her daughter in Italy. If convicted, her sentence is likely to be very high; as such, it constitutes a significant incentive to flee. I deny your application for your client to be released from custody.'

The court clerk, who was sitting next to the judge at a small table, typed two sentences on her computer.

'Do you wish to make any further applications, Dr Schlesinger?' asked the judge.

'I apply for a review of the custody order during the oral proceedings, and to be appointed as defence counsel in this case. Please could you also record my request to access the case files?'

'Did you get all that?' the judge asked the clerk. She nodded. The judge then dictated: 'Agreed and proclaimed: Dr Schlesinger is assigned to the accused as her defence counsel in these proceedings.' The clerk printed out a sheet of paper, which the judge signed.

'I've already spoken to the public prosecutor in question,' he told Schlesinger. 'You can have the case files right now.' The judge turned to the officer. 'Please take the accused away.'

'May I make a personal observation?' asked the judge, when he and Schlesinger were alone again.

'Of course,' said Schlesinger.

'We've known each other a long time now. Please don't take this the wrong way, but you look dreadful and reek of alcohol. You really should eat properly and get some sleep.'

'Thanks,' said Schlesinger. He put the case files under his arm, said goodbye, and took a taxi back to his chambers. By now it was half past three in the morning.

Schlesinger knew the man standing in the doorway of his apartment building. His name was Yasser, an elegantly dressed Algerian who worked as a debt collector and heavy. Schlesinger had defended him a few years earlier. Yasser had been accused of injuring three Russian bodyguards so badly at a nightclub that they had been hospitalised for weeks. Each of the three men was twice Yasser's size. They'd had knives, tasers and baseball bats, and Yasser just a ball-point pen. Yasser was remanded in custody because the clubgoers said he'd attacked first. Later, during the trial, the three Russians unexpectedly testified that they had started the fight. Yasser was acquitted.

'Hello, Yasser,' said Schlesinger.

'I'm sorry, Mr Lawyer,' said Yasser. He was wearing thin leather gloves. 'It's the Chinese. You know the rules.'

'Yes,' said Schlesinger.

'Do you have the money you owe them?'

'No.'

'Are you drunk?' asked Yasser.

'No, not even that. I was at the court.'

'This is going to hurt,' said Yasser. Then he punched Schlesinger hard in the stomach. As he doubled over, Yasser brought up his knee, smashed his nose and landed two simultaneous blows on his kidneys. Schlesinger went down on the floor.

'I'm sorry,' said Yasser.

'OK,' said Schlesinger. There was blood on his face and his nose was broken. He knew that it wasn't over yet. Yasser would take a photo once he had finished and send it to the Chinese. They were always mistrustful and wanted proof of everything. Yasser kicked Schlesinger in the face. He lost consciousness.

Schlesinger woke up on the sofa in his chambers. A knotted tea towel of ice cubes lay on his face, water was dripping into his ears, and the front of his jumper was wet. Yasser emerged from the kitchenette with a cup of coffee. He pulled up a chair to the sofa and sat down next to Schlesinger.

'Your office doesn't look too great,' said Yasser.

Schlesinger tried to work himself into an upright position. He couldn't.

'Best to stay lying down,' said Yasser. He drank some coffee. 'I like you very much, Mr Lawyer. But you've got to pay up. Next time, the Chinese want me to cut off a toe. And that's the way it'll keep going. Toes, fingers, a hand. Well, you know how it is . . .'

'I know, Yasser.'

'I once saw a film whose characters kept saying *It's nothing personal*. I don't get that. I mean, the whole of life is *personal*. All the same, I have nothing against you.'

'I know.'

34

'Can you raise the money?' asked Yasser.

'I think so,' said Schlesinger.

'I can only give you a week,' said Yasser. 'Understand?'

Schlesinger nodded.

'Repeat it.'

'One week,' said Schlesinger. He was afraid of losing consciousness again.

'You need to stop drinking.' Yasser got up and put his coffee cup on the chair.

Schlesinger closed his eyes.

'I've put the files on your desk. I took a look at them while you were out of it.'

Schlesinger knew that Yasser could barely read. He was a smart guy, but he had never been to school.

'It's the wrong side,' said Yasser.

Schlesinger didn't understand what he meant. He needed to sleep. Yasser put his coat on.

'Get the money to the Chinese as soon as you have it. Or call me. You've got my number,' he said.

Schlesinger heard Yasser pull the door shut from the outside. Then he fell asleep.

The next morning he drove himself to A&E. His head, torso and kidneys were X-rayed. He'd been lucky, the doctor said. They gave him some painkillers, and put dressings on his nose and the laceration on his forehead.

Schlesinger drove to a pawnbroker's and hocked the watch that his wife had given him for their tenth wedding anniversary. Then he went to the Chinese restaurant and paid off his debts. The Chinese man counted the money three times, put it in his pocket, and handed Schlesinger his IOU. 'Come back again soon,' he said. 'You're always welcome here.'

Schlesinger spent the rest of the day on the sofa. It was only in the evening that he got up, sat at his desk and tried to read through the files. The letters swam in front of his eyes. Schlesinger knew just how quickly a life could tip. This brief was his last chance. *Of course*, he thought, *I'm just the randomly appointed defence counsel, but it's a real case and I could win it*. He took two more painkillers, pulled on an old pair of jeans and a T-shirt, and cleaned the office until five in the morning. He poured the bottles of schnapps down the sink, gathered up all the rubbish, and took five big bags out to the bins. He hoovered the floor, cleaned the bathroom and the kitchenette, and put his dirty laundry into two suitcases to take to the cleaner's. Then he sorted out the pile of paperwork on his desk and lay back down on the sofa for a few hours.

The next day he drove to the detention centre. His client was shocked by his appearance, but he told her it wasn't so bad; he'd been in a car accident. He read her the contents of the investigation files. Every detail was incriminating. Her husband's business had been in debt. He had lost money speculating on options and shares. He hadn't been able to keep up payments on the bank loans, and their apartment was mortgaged to the hilt. When their finances collapsed, he couldn't cope; the responsibility for the business had 'done him in', the client said. They had quarrelled more frequently as a result. The gun: yes, she had got it from her father. He had shown her how to look after it. After her father died, she had cleaned the gun a few times and put it away in a bedroom drawer. That's exactly what she had told the police, and that's all she knew.

Schlesinger went to a copy shop and had the photos from the case files enlarged. He stuck them on the walls of his office and stared at them for hours on end. He didn't understand what Yasser could have meant. He read the files over and over again until he knew them practically off by heart. He tried to find a hole in the evidence, an angle for the defence, some kind of way out. After three weeks he gave up. Outside, it had turned cold; the grey days of Berlin's winter were under way. Schlesinger pulled on his coat and headed to the Chinese. He wanted to gamble and drink again, and to forget who he had become.

Yasser was standing in front of the restaurant door.

'You don't want to go in there,' said Yasser.

'I do,' said Schlesinger.

'Are you giving up again?'

'My client did it. She shot her husband in the back of the head. There's no other explanation. We're going to lose.'

Yasser shook his head. 'You're an idiot, Mr Lawyer. Come on,' he said.

'Where to?'

'We're going for dinner and you're paying.'

They climbed into Yasser's Bentley and drove to the most expensive fish restaurant on the Kurfürstendamm. Yasser ordered oysters and white wine, Schlesinger just a fish soup.

'The oysters here are fresh and extremely good,' said Yasser. 'The owner buys them down at the Großmarkt at three in the morning. You like oysters?'

'No,' said Schlesinger.

'Try one anyway.'

'I'd rather not.'

Yasser placed an oyster on a side plate and pushed it across the table. 'Eat,' he said.

'It tastes of salt, cold fish and metal,' said Schlesinger. He felt like spitting the oyster out again.

'You should drink some white wine with it,' said Yasser. 'Do you still drink?'

'Well, not as much, at least,' said Schlesinger.

'Good,' said Yasser, and continued to eat in silence. When he had finished, he said: 'It's the wrong side, Mr Lawyer. Very simple.'

'You already told me that, but I don't understand,' said Schlesinger. '*What's* the fucking wrong side?'

Yasser leaned forward a little. 'You're paying for the meal?'

'Yes,' said Schlesinger.

An hour later, Yasser dropped him back at his chambers. Schlesinger immediately lay down on the sofa, and for the first time since he had taken on the case he slept for twelve hours straight.

~

Eight months later, the trial began. The newspapers covered it extensively, the public was certain of the accused's guilt, and the prosecutor gave endless interviews.

The investigators had found a witness who reported seeing the couple arguing loudly in a supermarket the day before the crime. The broker who had arranged the man's life insurance said that he must have been 'under a lot of pressure'; he was 'really nervous'. The police stated that the accused's manner had been 'strikingly cold', and a psychiatric expert was of the view that she was 'fully capable of the crime'.

Schlesinger sat quietly next to his client during the trial. He did not put any questions or make any applications to the court.

On the morning of the fifth day, the presiding judge said: 'According to the witness list, we're only due to hear from the firearms expert today. That will complete the presentation of evidence to the court. Are there any further applications from the parties to the case? From you, Counsel for the Defence?'

Schlesinger shook his head. The judge raised his eyebrows.

'Very well. Please call the expert witness,' he said to the court officer.

The expert took his place in the witness chair and confirmed his personal details. The judge told him that he was obliged to tell the truth.

'If I'm reading this correctly, you work at the Forensic Science Institute,' said the judge.

'Yes, in the fields of firearms identification, ballistics, and weapons and ammunition technology.'

'You've examined the weapon and the ammunition in this case?' asked the judge.

'That's correct.'

'What can you tell us about the weapon?'

'It's a pistol, a model called FN Browning HP. It was manufactured by the Fabrique Nationale company in Herstal in Belgium. It's one of the most widely used pistols of all time, adopted by the police and the military in over fifty countries. It's been in production since 1935.'

'Was the bullet in the victim's head fired from this weapon? And does the cartridge case found at the crime scene originate from this weapon and bullet?' asked the judge.

'We fired the Hi-Power—'

'The High Power?' interrupted the judge.

'This Browning is also known as the Hi-Power. That's what the "HP" stands for in its name.'

'Thank you, please continue.'

'We fired the weapon into a four-metre-long water tank. That way we could recover the ammunition without it having been contaminated. Then we compared the ammunition components with the cartridge case found at the scene and the bullet from the victim's head.'

'How did you go about that?'

'When a gun is fired, a set of markings are scored into the metal of the cartridge case and the bullet. These markings are caused by the firing action and by the barrel of the gun. It's important to be aware that the interiors of modern gun barrels aren't smooth. They have spiral-shaped grooves designed to spin the projectile, in order to improve the stability of its flight. And these "lands and grooves" are later visible on the bullet as a set of impressions. The impact of the firing pin, traces of the action face, and the imprint of the ejector can also be seen on the base of the cartridge casing. We examine these impressions using a comparison microscope. If that's insufficient and we're still unsure, we can examine the traces with a scanning electron microscope. But that wasn't necessary here.'

'In this instance, what did your investigations show?' asked the judge.

'I can say with certainty that the bullet in the victim's head and the cartridge case came from the weapon found at the crime scene. I can explain in further detail if you'd like.'

'Thanks, I think I've got it,' said the judge. 'Are there any other questions for the expert witness?'

The public prosecutor shook her head.

'In that case, you may step down,' said the judge.

'No, not just yet,' said Schlesinger. 'I have some questions.'

'Forgive me,' said the judge. He looked surprised. 'You haven't asked any questions up until now, Dr Schlesinger, so I ... Very well, your questions please.'

'May I show two photographic enlargements to the court? They'll make it easier for everyone concerned to follow what the expert witness is saying. I'm referring to photograph Number Fourteen and photograph Number Fifteen in the visual evidence folder.' Schlesinger had arranged for each of the photos to be mounted on cardboard.

'Yes, please go ahead,' said the judge.

Schlesinger got up and placed the photographs on a display stand. He angled it so that the judges and the spectators were able to see.

'This is the back of the dead man's head, where the bullet penetrated,' he said, and pointed at the first photo. 'In the course of the trial, we've heard from a medical expert that this is known as a "contact shot". You can see a small, black circle on the skin around the entry wound. This circle, we were told, is created by the hot gunshot residue that exits the muzzle when the weapon is fired. The residue is deposited around the circumference of the entry wound if the muzzle comes into contact with the head, or if the weapon is held only a couple of centimetres away from it. Is that correct?'

'I can confirm that,' said the expert witness. 'The photo undoubtedly shows it was a contact shot.'

'But this isn't an appropriate question for an expert in firearms technology,' interjected the public prosecutor. 'Besides, as you yourself have said, we've already heard all this from the medical expert.'

'Please be patient,' said Schlesinger. 'I haven't asked my main question yet.'

Schlesinger pointed at the second image.

'Here's one of the photos your colleagues took of the location where the body was found. A meadow by the lake. The meadow, as we heard during the trial, had been mowed shortly before the crime took place. The dead man is lying on his front. Are you with me so far?' asked Schlesinger.

'Yes,' said the expert witness.

'Were you aware of these photographs when you wrote up your report?'

'No. My task was purely to examine the bullet, the cartridge case and the gun, and those items were sent to me. I've never seen these photos before. But they're also irrelevant to my investigation.'

'I agree – completely irrelevant, as are your questions,' said the public prosecutor. 'Where are you going with this?'

'Please stop interrupting,' said Schlesinger. He turned again to the expert witness. 'In the photograph, you can see a couple of little markers, numbered One and Two. Number One is where the pistol was found; Number Two is where the cartridge case was discovered.'

'From what I can tell from the photo, that's probably the Browning I examined,' said the expert witness.

'That's what the police report says as well.' Schlesinger turned to face the presiding judge. 'May I have the weapon for a moment?'

The judge got up and went over to a shelf behind the judges' bench. He took the pistol from a cardboard box. It was in a clear plastic bag.

'It's already been examined, of course,' said the judge as he took out the gun and handed it to Schlesinger.

'Thank you,' said Schlesinger, and placed the pistol on the table in front of the expert witness. 'Is this the weapon?'

The expert witness picked up the pistol while looking down at his report.

'Yes, the serial numbers match.'

'I'm not really au fait with these things. Please help me out. The opening on the right side of the barrel – what's it for?'

'It's called the ejection port.'

'Please explain to us how it works.'

'When a cartridge is fired, the slide of the gun recoils. In the process, a claw pulls the empty case out of the chamber. It hits a rigid metal part, the so-called "ejector", and is then thrown from the weapon's locking system.'

'In other words, the empty cartridge case flies sideways out of the gun.'

'Yes, that's one way of describing it.'

'And since the opening is on the right, that means the cartridge case is also ejected to the right.'

'Yes.'

'Can you tell us the velocity of the ejected case and how far it's able to travel?'

'No, you'd have to measure it.'

'Of course. But is it realistic to say that the cartridge case could travel a distance of around a metre?'

'Approximately, yes.'

'Good. That's what the literature on the subject says too.'

Schlesinger walked slowly across the courtroom, back to the enlargement.

'Your expert view is confirmed by this photograph. The cartridge case was actually found lying in the grass about a metre away from the weapon. It couldn't have ricocheted off anything – as we can see, there are no trees or other obstructions in the vicinity.'

'Right,' said the expert witness.

'But please now take a closer look,' said Schlesinger. 'Look again at this photograph.' His voice grew quieter. The judge, lay judges, and public prosecutor all turned their heads to look at the display stand with the photos. Schlesinger waited a moment. Then he said: 'Do you see? The cartridge case wasn't found to the right of the body. It was lying a metre away from it – but on the left side.'

'That's . . .' said the public prosecutor in a low voice, leafing through her files.

Schlesinger walked back to his seat.

'If the man had indeed been shot from behind with this gun,' he said, 'then the cartridge case would have been found to the right of the body.'

'I would think so, yes,' said the expert witness.

'So how is it possible that it's lying on the left?' asked Schlesinger.

The expert witness gave the question some thought. Then he said: 'I can't explain it.'

'But there is actually a logical explanation,' said Schlesinger.

'There is?'

'The man shot himself.'

There was a murmur from the public gallery and the press. The presiding judge stopped taking notes. Everyone stared at Schlesinger.

'He made the mistake of holding the gun upside down – that's to say, with the bottom of the grip facing upwards. And because he did that, the cartridge case was ejected to the left. There's practically no other way of holding a pistol if you want to shoot yourself in the back of the head. It's unbelievably difficult.'

Schlesinger paused again. For a second time, the expert witness picked up the gun that was on the table before him. He pulled back the slide to make sure the barrel was empty. Then he put the weapon to the back of his head. In the process, he rotated the gun in such a way that its grip was facing upwards.

'You're right,' said the expert witness. 'It's practically the only way to hold it.'

'Exactly,' said Schlesinger. He turned to the judges and lay judges. 'So this man tried to fake his own murder. His motive is also plain, given everything we've learned in this trial: he wanted his wife to get the life insurance payout.'

~

Schlesinger's client was acquitted the following day. The presiding judge said that the police had assumed from the start it was murder, and had therefore failed to investigate any other alternative. The proceedings had been shaped by a long series of hasty assumptions, and each piece of evidence could be interpreted differently. On the basis of the available evidence, the possibility that the man had killed himself could thus not be excluded.

The public prosecutor did not appeal against the judgement.

After the acquittal Schlesinger treated Yasser to another meal. Yasser made him relate the whole of the trial; he wanted to know every detail.

When he had finished, Schlesinger asked: 'How did you spot it so quickly?'

'Mr Lawyer,' said Yasser, 'you don't want to know.'

A Light Blue Day

She killed her child, the judge says when delivering the verdict; of that the court has no doubt. The infant had cried day and night, and she had been unable to bear it any longer. She had slammed the back of his head against the wall four times and he had died from his brain injuries.

The judge keeps saying 'infant' and 'child', but she had given her baby a name. Not Jonas or Kevin like everyone else, but a really lovely name she'd once seen in a magazine: Ryan. The judge sits in his chair and announces the verdict, and everyone in the courtroom thinks this is her story. But there's a whole other story she can't tell right now.

The judge says that she was 'suffering from diminished responsibility at the time of the crime'. Her husband had left her alone with the child and the situation had 'completely overwhelmed' her.

She is sentenced to three and a half years in prison.

The tabloids say this is too lenient and dub her the 'Monster Mother'.

The public prosecutor's office does not lodge an appeal, and the judgment becomes legally binding.

There's no alcohol in prison. She stops smoking, too, because she has no money. She's woken every morning at six, and work starts at seven. She sorts screws into sets, glues chocolate boxes, or assembles rubber seals. All the women wear identical blue aprons.

After a year she gets a job in the carpentry workshop. This is better. Now she builds benches and tables for the courts and the prison. She's skilful, and the head of the workshop likes her. 'I'm only just getting my head straight,' she tells him. She makes a little walnut box with a birch inlay. It's put at the very front of the workshop's display case, where everyone can see it.

After a year and a half, she's granted overnight release for the first time. She has permission to leave the prison and to spend the night at home. She tells the head warden that she would rather come back that evening instead.

She takes the bus to the city centre and walks along the high street. It's a light blue day, just as it was that day. There are people sitting in cafés. She looks around the shops and buys herself a silk scarf with her prison allowance. She had forgotten how much life there is out here. She walks on a bit further to the park and lies on the grass in the sunshine. She props herself up on her elbows and watches the people strolling by. There's a boy of maybe four or five. He's holding an ice cream that's as big as his face. His father kneels down in front of him and wipes his mouth with a tissue.

She gets up, pulls the silk scarf from her neck, throws it in a bin, and heads back to the prison.

Six months later, she's released. At home, she finds her husband sitting on the sofa. He didn't come to pick her up, even though she had written to him. Her letter is on the kitchen table. The paper is dirty and marked with beer-bottle rings.

'Why didn't you ever visit me?' she asks.

He picks up a lighter from the table and plays around with it. He doesn't look at her.

'The TV's broken,' he says.

'OK,' she says.

'The guy from the repair shop says it's a problem with the dish. I've bought a new one.'

He keeps playing with the lighter.

'I'll sort it out now,' he says, and gets up.

He carries the box containing the new satellite dish out onto the balcony and rips it open. Gets the toolbox from the kitchen. Pushes the garden chair against the wall and uses it as a ladder. It's not high enough. He stands with one foot on the back of the chair and the other on the balcony railing.

'Pass me the red screwdriver,' he says.

'OK,' she says.

She digs around in the toolbox and gives him the red screwdriver. He tries to remove the old screws from the wall.

'They're stuck,' he says.

She had been shopping that day. Just for half an hour. When she came back, he was sitting on the bedroom floor. It wasn't his fault, he said, the kid had slipped out of his hands. They'd send him down for *life* because he had priors for robbery and assault; he knew those judges. She laid her son, who was now dead, on her lap and kissed him. He had such a beautiful face.

'You didn't even come to the trial,' she says.

He looks down at her from above. His shirt is hanging out of his trousers; his stomach is all hairy.

That day, he had told her she should admit responsibility, that it would be better for everyone. *Admit responsibility* – he never normally used that kind of phrase. She should have noticed.

He has another go at the screws.

'They're broken,' he says. 'Rusted.'

She'd only get a light sentence, he had said, and the women's prison wasn't so bad. They could stay together, a family. 'A family,' she had kept on repeating, while Ryan lay in her lap, dead. She didn't know that he had slammed the baby's head against the wall. She had believed him. Then.

'I've been so stupid,' she says now.

She kicks the chair. His mouth opens. She sees his stubble, his yellow teeth, his water-blue eyes, the ones she used to love. He loses his footing, tips backwards and falls. It's four storeys. He slams onto the concrete. The impact ruptures his right heart valve; a rib punctures his aorta; he bleeds out into his body. She walks slowly down the flights of stairs. She stands next to him on the pavement and waits until he is dead.

The investigation is led by the same public prosecutor who took part in her first trial. He's now a senior public prosecutor and has grown a moustache. He thinks that she killed her husband as well.

She's learned a few things in prison and refuses to answer the questions put to her by the police. All she says is that she wants to see a lawyer. An officer takes her back to her cell.

The following day, the judge remands her in custody. The evidence gathered is thin, but the judge wants to give the homicide unit more time.

The police question the neighbours. Nobody heard them arguing. An old man saw them on the balcony but couldn't make out any detail. Another witness says that she stood 'stiffly' next to her husband as he lay on the street.

According to the pathologist's report, the deceased was intoxicated and all of his injuries were consistent with a fall. 'From a forensic point of view, there is no evidence of death being caused by another person's hand.'

Ten days later, a hearing is held to review the custody order. She continues to say nothing, just as her lawyer has advised. The senior public prosecutor is convinced that she did it, but says he can't prove it. The judge nods and revokes the custody order.

She leaves the courtroom with her lawyer. Once they're through the door she feels compelled to tell him everything. She can't stay silent any longer; she has to 'get it out'. She's not sure whether it was revenge or something else for which she doesn't have the words. She isn't sorry. 'Do you understand?' she asks the lawyer.

She walks with him to the lobby. She stops in front of a bench, kneels down, and looks under the seat. 'It's one of mine,' she says. 'This is a very good bench.'

Lydia

'I've met another man,' says Meyerbeck's wife. It's Sunday morning. There's an untouched bread roll on her plate. Meyerbeck, on the other hand, is feeling hungry. His wife talks very quickly while he eats. Meyerbeck has had a stutter since childhood. He can only speak fluently when no one is listening.

We could drive out to the lake today, Meyerbeck thinks. His wife would read her magazines and he would look at the sky. At the lake, everything would be the same as it had always been. Later, they'd go to the pizzeria and have a cold beer outside.

His wife says that she couldn't help it, and then she starts to cry. They've been together a long time. Meyerbeck stands up. He puts his hands in his pockets and looks out of the kitchen window.

~

Four months later Meyerbeck moves out – a fourth-floor apartment; two rooms with a kitchen, bathroom and balcony. His wife, who is now no longer his wife, has liaised with his new landlord, changed their bank account details and put up a new nameplate by his doorbell. The first night, he opens the cupboards in the kitchen and looks at the crockery she's bought him. There's a lot of crockery. Meyerbeck sits down on a chair. He's smoking again, like he did before he got married.

It isn't far from the apartment to the company where Meyerbeck has worked for the last thirteen years. Two stops on the S-Bahn and a short walk. His office is next to the server room. It's air-conditioned – no windows, just a skylight. Although he's the company's best programmer, he turned down a promotion to departmental head. Meyerbeck doesn't get along with other people very well; he prefers to be given his work assignments in written form.

He eats in the company canteen every lunchtime now. The only time he used to go there was for the office Christmas party. The room's high ceiling makes it echo and it's too loud for him. In the evening, he mostly eats in a fast-food restaurant. At home, he watches TV. At weekends, he sometimes goes to see a film. He doesn't drive out to the lake anymore.

On his forty-fifth birthday, his wife sends him a text message and he gets a computer-generated card from his bank. At work, his boss gives him some supermarket chocolates. She asks him whether he is lonely. 'Always alone, Mr Meyerbeck – that's no good,' she says. Meyerbeck doesn't reply.

～

One Sunday evening, Meyerbeck sees a report on television about sex dolls. While the programme's still on, he opens his laptop and finds the manufacturer's website. He stays up until five in the morning reading customer reviews on a forum.

The following day, he's barely able to concentrate at work and leaves earlier than usual. On his laptop at home, Meyerbeck repeatedly assembles new dolls. Face, breast size, skin tone (from 'pale' to 'cocoa'), lip colour ('apricot', 'pink', 'red', 'bronze', 'natural'), nail colour, eyes, hair. There are eleven different types of vagina. For the first time, he calls in sick. He sleeps for a few hours, and when he wakes up, he knows the doll's name: Lydia.

*   *   *

Eight weeks later, Meyerbeck takes a day off. The package is delivered in the early afternoon. He signs the courier's device and drags the box into the apartment.

The doll is wrapped in soft cloth. He's glad that she's wearing underwear. She is heavy – almost fifty kilos. He lifts her out of the box, sits her on the sofa, fetches his dressing gown, and drapes it over her shoulders. He goes into the kitchen and closes the door behind him. He's read up on everything about her. She has a steel skeleton that 'does not allow unnatural contortions'. Her skin requires a regular, light application of powder to keep it 'supple' and 'lifelike'. After an hour, Meyerbeck goes back into the living room. He doesn't look at the doll. He flattens the box so he can take it out to the bins. At the front door, he doubles back and switches on the television.

Ten days after Lydia's arrival, Meyerbeck sleeps with her for the first time. Three weeks later he orders some clothes for her on the internet – lingerie, shoes, nightgowns and a scarf. Meyerbeck learns how to cook so that he doesn't have to go to the restaurant in the evenings; he wants to be with her. He often watches romantic films with her now. He thinks about her at work, and buys her flowers every Monday. In the evenings, he tells her about his day. After a few weeks, he's able to talk to her without stuttering. He buys an exercise bike so he can stay in shape. When he lies in bed with her at night, he talks about the future, about the house he wants to buy so that she can sit out in the garden in the sun without anyone disturbing her.

~

On a mild, late-summer afternoon, Meyerbeck takes off his tie in the street and undoes the top button of his shirt. In the old days, he'd never have done such a thing. A couple of days earlier, he'd bought Lydia a bottle of champagne and twelve roses. It was her birthday: she has been with him for twelve months now. It's been a good year, he thinks.

The balcony door of his apartment has been forced open. The doll is lying over the back of the living-room sofa. Dress and underwear are torn, the head rotated 180 degrees, the legs spread wide. Candles from Meyerbeck's candleholder have been inserted into the mouth, anus and vagina. On the table, written in the lipstick he'd bought for her, are the words *perverted pig*.

Meyerbeck knows immediately that it was his neighbour. He's often caught him leaning over the balcony trying to look into his apartment.

He removes the candles. Carefully, he turns Lydia's head and legs back to a neutral position. He feels her body like a doctor; he wants to know if any part of her skeleton has been broken. He carries her in his arms to the bathroom, lays her in the bathtub and runs some water. He bathes her for two hours, talking gently to her all the while. He cleans her with a soft sponge, rinses out her orifices, washes and dries her hair. Every now and again he leaves the bathroom so she won't see him crying. Then he lifts her out of the bath, towels her dry and carries her to the bed. He powders her skin carefully while stroking her. He dresses her in a nightgown, lays the duvet over her and turns out the light.

Back in the living room, he stuffs the torn clothing and the candles into a bin bag. He cleans the living-room table until there's no longer any trace of lipstick. He nails the balcony door shut.

That night, Meyerbeck sleeps on the sofa. He gets up a number of times to check on Lydia. He sits on a chair by the bed and holds her hand.

The next morning, he calls the office and says that he needs to take some leave; a family emergency. He spends the next few days at Lydia's side. He moves the TV into the bedroom and reads aloud to her from books.

~

Four weeks later, Meyerbeck's neighbour is taken to A&E. Two of his ribs and his left collarbone are broken. His testicles are bruised and his front teeth have been knocked out. A laceration above his right eyebrow needs eight stitches. The doctor's report says that he was found outside his apartment and that a neighbour called the ambulance.

The police go to the man's address and question all the neighbours. When they ring Meyerbeck's bell, he answers the door but says nothing. He hands them a plastic bag containing a baseball bat smeared with blood. The police handcuff Meyerbeck and press him to the ground. He offers no resistance. When the officers are sure that he presents no danger, he's allowed to sit up. In the bedroom, they find the doll lying on the bed. Meyerbeck is taken to the police station.

An hour later, a policewoman tries to question him. By now she knows that he has no previous criminal convictions, and that he has a steady job and is divorced. He bought the baseball bat on the internet; the receipt was still in the bag. The policewoman gives Meyerbeck time. He stutters so badly that he can hardly say his name. She asks him what his doll is called. He looks up for the first time. 'Lydia,' he says. Things get easier after that.

The public prosecutor charges Meyerbeck with grievous bodily harm. The case is heard before a judge and two lay judges ten months after the crime. *Every word counts now*, thinks Meyerbeck. He discussed it all with Lydia, practised in front of her again and again, but now he can't get even the simplest sentence out. He just nods when the presiding judge asks if the accusation made against him is true. The neighbour has submitted a doctor's note stating that he's ill and won't be able to attend. The only witness heard in court is the policewoman. She describes the investigation and Meyerbeck's police interview. He had admitted everything straight away; she did not think he was mentally ill. 'He's just a lonely man,' she says.

The court has engaged a psychiatric expert. The presiding judge asks him if Meyerbeck is dangerous.

'It's strange to love dolls,' says the psychiatrist, 'but not dangerous.'

'Is it common?' asks the presiding judge.

'Over the past twenty years,' says the expert, 'an industry has emerged that manufactures silicon humanoid dolls with steel or aluminium skeletons. These dolls cost between 3,500 and 15,000 euros. They're made in Russia, Germany, France, Japan, the UK and America. Soon they'll have inbuilt computers so they can talk. There's no definitive scholarly study as yet, but according to the literature, the typical buyer is white, single, heterosexual, and between forty and sixty-five years old. The dolls are usually promoted on the manufacturers' websites as masturbation and sex objects, but the owners often have a relationship with the dolls that goes far beyond the sexual. They become life partners for some. In Japan, there's even a funeral ceremony for dolls when their owners marry real people.'

Meyerbeck sees the public prosecutor shaking her head.

'Agalmatophilia – that's to say, the love of statues and dolls – is a fetish. We use the term to describe a sexual attraction to inanimate objects,' says the psychiatrist.

'Is that enough for these men?' asks the presiding judge. 'After all, a doll can't return their love.'

'Falling in love is a very complex process. Initially, we're not in love with the partner themselves, but with the image we create of them. The critical phase of every relationship begins when reality catches up with this image, when we recognise who the other person really is,' says the expert witness. 'In the States, there are numerous marriages between prison inmates and normal women leading full and active lives. The women usually meet the men through personal ads, so they know they'll probably never live with their partners. Nevertheless, the relationships are stable. It's the same phenomenon in Mr Meyerbeck's case. The woman's love for the prisoner is never tested by reality. The relationship between Mr Meyerbeck and his doll can't become real either. His feelings of love will thus presumably remain stable. It's an enduringly happy relationship.'

Meyerbeck is given a suspended sentence of six months. The presiding judge says that everyone is free to live their lives as they see fit, and that it's none of the state's business as long as no one is harmed. 'However, we must pass judgement on you for the offence you committed. We are satisfied that you viewed the damage done to your doll as an attack on your life partner. We do not think that you are more dangerous than any other man whose wife has been raped. But even if Lydia were a real person, your actions would not be justified. You may only claim to have acted in self-defence if an attack takes place in the present moment or if it is imminent. But as your neighbour's actions had long since taken place, the use of self-defence as a mitigating factor was not an option anymore. What you carried out, therefore, was an act of revenge – a motive we're able to understand, but which our legal system does not permit.'

~

At home, Meyerbeck draws the curtains in order to be alone with Lydia. A suspended sentence isn't so bad, he says to her. He tells her about the trial, about the presiding judge and about the fear he'd felt. Sometime later, her head rests on his shoulder. *An enduringly happy relationship*, he thinks. Meyerbeck is sure he did the right thing. It was necessary, no matter what the judge said.

And then they go to sleep.

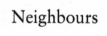

Neighbours

In the morning, eyes still closed, he feels for his wife's hand. For twenty-four years, his days have begun like this; they've spent only a few nights apart. She always grips his hand while half asleep, a reflex like a baby's.

The other side of the bed is empty. He had forgotten again in his sleep. Brinkmann sits up and turns on the light. Emily was fifty-three years old when she discovered black spots on her lower legs: skin cancer. The tumour had spread, the doctors said, with metastases in the lymph nodes, the lungs, the liver – so-called daughter tumours. There was no point in operating. After a month, she went into hospital. Her face on the white pillow, getting smaller week by week. Before she died, she regained consciousness one last time. He bent over the bed and she grasped his head with both hands. She couldn't speak. He saw her fear.

An hour and a half later a machine sounded an alarm; two nurses rolled her bed out of the room, knocking its edge on the door frame. He was told that he couldn't go with them. And then nothing happened for a long time.

The next morning a young doctor came to the room. 'Your wife has died,' he said. It had been painless. But that was a lie. Brinkmann packed the things from the hospital cupboard in her red-and-white-checked suitcase: her pyjamas, her cosmetics, her hairbrush. The books she hadn't managed to read. He would have liked to discuss it all with her. In their first apartment they had shared a desk – his half, her half. They had never stopped talking to each other.

At home, he removed the post from the letter box. He waited in the hallway with her suitcase and the letters with her name on them. He waited for something to happen, but nothing happened. He sat down on the chair beside the umbrella stand and phoned his daughters. They wanted to come right away. There was no need, he said, he was fine. He stayed up until dawn; he wanted to be awake and to wait for Emily.

* * *

Two days later, he saw her one last time in the hospital. Her face was neither severe nor beautiful. The pain, the joy, the goodness had vanished. He had her cremated because that was what she'd wanted. *Death isn't a mystery we have to kneel down before*, he thought at the funeral. In the weeks and months after her death he dreamed of her voice. Nothing seemed meaningful anymore.

All that was four years ago. Brinkmann makes himself coffee in the kitchen in his dressing gown, and goes out into the garden with his cup. It's still dark. He looks at the blurry lights of the container ships and the pleasure craft. Later, in the shower, he feels dizzy. He leans against the wall and closes his eyes until it passes. He shaves, gets dressed and polishes his shoes. He's scared of falling out of time.

He puts on his coat, picks up his keys and leaves the house. At the kiosk, the elderly owner sits behind the counter and knits. Emily always found this old lady amusing. They had imagined children and grand-children and great-grandchildren with entire closets full of knitwear made from coarse wool.

He buys a newspaper and some cigarettes. A convertible drives slowly past him; a young woman has leaned her head against the side window and is sleeping. *The driver's being careful*, Brinkman thinks, *he doesn't want to wake her. Maybe they're coming back from a party out in the country; they left at dawn, and later he'll take her to bed.* Brinkmann's stomach contracts. He walks down the many steps to the shore, past the two-storey houses and pretty front gardens until he reaches the café. He orders a small breakfast. Then he reads the paper for two hours. Every now and then, he observes the couple at the next table: the man is tapping on his mobile phone, the woman gazes out at the river. Brinkmann had come here even as a child. Back then, his father had brought him along; boat pilots and boatmen had sat on the beach at night, drinking. He pays and walks back home. As always, he counts the 136 steps up to the street. He's out of breath when he reaches the top. The rest of the day still lies before him, barren and empty. Like every single day since Emily's death.

~

His daughters give him a Caribbean cruise for his birthday. He doesn't know what to do with himself on the ship. The entertainment, the water slides, the formal dinners in huge salons – he finds it all repulsive. He spends most of his time in the cabin. On his birthday, the ship's staff arrange a table with flowers and presents for him; he feels embarrassed. Women approach him, but he declines any further contact.

When he gets back from the cruise, the house next door has been sold. A dark green car stands in front of the garage, a 1960s open-top Jaguar. A few days later, one of the new neighbours rings the doorbell. She gives just her first name: Antonia. She has brought him a Madeira cake – 'Baked with my own two hands,' she says. Brinkman invites her in. He makes some coffee and they sit in the garden. They'd been so happy to finally find a house in the area – you hardly ever saw anything for sale here on the Elbchaussee. 'We looked for ages,' she says. She touches Brinkmann twice, on his forearm, his hand. He tries to listen to what she's saying, but can't concentrate. She leaves after half an hour; the back of her dress is cut low. At the garden gate she briefly turns again. She looks like Emily, he thinks: the same high cheekbones, the same laugh, the elegant posture. 'Why don't you drop by sometime? I'd like that,' she says.

*　　*　　*

Then it is summer. Next door, they renovate the pool, install underwater lighting and lay flagstones in neutral tones. Brinkmann looks out onto the blue-green water from his terrace at night.

On the first really hot day he goes to a deli and buys two bottles of the white wine Emily liked. He rings the neighbours' doorbell. Antonia opens the door wearing light-coloured shorts and a white T-shirt. She's not wearing a bra; her legs are tanned and smooth.

Brinkmann has never been to this house before, a 1920s U-shaped bungalow whose inner courtyard opens onto the river. She gives him a tour and shows him the new pool. Then she gets two ice-filled glasses from the kitchen and they drink the wine. She's full of life, he thinks. He sits in the half-shade and tells her about the cruise. She laughs a lot, her bright, happy laugh. Does he fancy a swim, she asks? It's so refreshing and it would do him good. He doesn't want her to see his body, his white chest hair, the age spots. 'The chlorine doesn't agree with me,' he says.

Sweat gathers in his eyebrows. He says he needs to go to the bathroom. She describes the way through the house: down the hall, third door on the left.

On the shelf above the washbasin are perfume bottles, glycerine soaps from Sicily, and a large shell. He runs his fingers over the inside; it's pink, smooth and warm. Brinkmann bends his head in the sink and lets cold water run over his neck until he feels better. When he returns, she's sitting at the edge of the pool, her feet in the water. The sun is unbearably hot.

'It's going to be a nice summer,' she says, leaning her head back.

'I'm afraid I have to go now,' he says.

Later, from his terrace, he sees her reclining on the yellow lilo in the pool, one hand in the water, eyes closed. Her body glistens with suntan oil.

Brinkmann visits Antonia nearly every day. In the morning he has breakfast at the café, at lunchtime he goes over to hers. He always takes little gifts along – sweets, magazines, books. They spend their days by the pool. Antonia says that she's glad he's here; he's such a good listener. She tells him about herself. Her parents are university lecturers and she's their only child. She talks a lot about her father, who is younger than Brinkmann. He's a quiet man, like Brinkmann; the author of a standard work on Renaissance Florence, she says. As a child, she often visited the city with him, walking for hours through museums and churches. She met her husband while she was a student. Marriage, she says, was a release. She couldn't bear men any longer – her wedding ring shielded her from them. She lies naked on the flagstones next to the pool and he pretends it means nothing. *That's the agreement*, he thinks.

Her husband usually stays late at the agency and gives her a call before he leaves. Brinkmann never meets him. At the weekend, he sometimes sees the neighbour fixing his car; he's set up a workshop in the garage. It relaxes him, says Antonia when he asks her about it.

~

Midsummer. She goes to visit her parents for a week. Three days after her departure, on a Sunday, the Jaguar is standing in the neighbours' driveway, raised up on two jacks. Tools lie on the concrete and the lawn. The car's front wheels have been removed and are propped against the wall of the house. The neighbour is lying under the engine. Brinkmann can see just his legs and his espadrilles.

'Good morning,' the man says. He rolls out on a board from under the car and gets up. His face and hands are covered in oil. 'I'd better not shake hands.'

He looks like an airline pilot, thinks Brinkmann.

'I've heard so much about you – Antonia talks about you all the time,' says the man. 'Pleased to meet you at last.' He points at the Jaguar. 'Damn car. The sump's cracked.'

'That's a very elegant car,' says Brinkmann. 'Have fun.'

'Enjoy the rest of your Sunday,' says the man, 'and hopefully see you soon.' He lies back down on the board and rolls himself under the engine.

Brinkmann puts his foot on the bumper. The chrome blinds him in the sunshine. He pushes against it with his full weight. The two jacks topple over, and the car slides onto the man.

It's a horrible death, a forensic pathologist will later tell the investigators, and it happens quite often. The immense pressure on the chest drives the blood into the head and feet. Thousands of capillaries burst; they look like tiny insect bites. The face swells and turns a dark violet-red. Screws, clamps and metal parts indent themselves on the skin. The victim suffocates.

Brinkmann turns and walks back to his house. He runs a hand lightly over the rhododendrons in the front garden. Emily planted them; autumn was the best time for that, she had said.

~

The funeral is two weeks later. It's held in the same church where the requiem Mass for Emily took place, and Brinkmann is wearing the same suit as he did then. He sits behind Antonia, who turns round to him several times.

In the weeks that follow he looks after her, helps her with the paperwork, drives her into the city, comforts her. They often have dinner together now; she still talks a lot about her husband. In the spring, Brinkmann suggests that she come with him to Sardinia; he has rented a house by the sea. 'It's best if you're not alone right now,' he says.

Brinkmann is never investigated. According to the police report, it was an accident. Only once, years later, on a summer afternoon, will he tell his lawyer about it. He'll say that he feels no remorse and no guilt; nothing troubles him, and he doesn't even sleep badly. And then the terrace door will open, and Antonia will ask if he fancies a dip in the pool, the water's lovely.

The Small Man

S trelitz is forty-three years old, single, no kids. And he's small. He has small hands, small feet and a small nose. He wears special elevator shoes that make him five centimetres taller. In his sitting room, there's a collection of biographies on small men: Napoleon, Caesar, Mussolini, the Marquis de Sade, Kant, Sartre, Capote, Karajan, Einstein. He's read every study going on small men. He knows that they have a higher life expectancy and more stable marriages, and that they're less prone to testicular cancer. He can list the heights of Tom Cruise (five feet seven inches), Dustin Hoffman (five feet six inches), and Prince (five feet three inches). He's seen every film starring Humphrey Bogart (five feet six inches), and has a photo of the actor on his bathroom mirror. He knows the two bits about Bogart's size from his favourite film, *The Big Sleep*, off by heart:

MARTHA VICKERS: You're not very tall, are you?

HUMPHREY BOGART: Well, I . . . try to be.

A few minutes later Bogart meets Lauren Bacall for the first time:

BACALL: So you're a private detective? I didn't know they existed, except in books – or else they were greasy little men snooping around hotel corridors. Why, you're a mess, aren't you?

BOGART: I'm not very tall, either. Next time I'll come on stilts, wear a white tie, and carry a tennis racket.

BACALL: I doubt if even that would help.

In the film, of course, Bogart gets the girl. But actually, thinks Strelitz, Bacall is right. Nothing helps. He's tried everything; women just don't find him attractive. He bought an expensive car way beyond his means, went to clubs and spent money on drinks and champagne – all without success. The women let him buy them drinks and then disappeared with other men. For a while, he focused on cultivated women. He took evening classes in Philosophy and Literature, went to book readings, to the theatre and the opera – again, nothing. He signed up to four dating sites simultaneously. Women liked his photos, and he had no problem communicating with them online. But as soon as he mentioned his size, they lost interest. If he kept it a secret and met a woman for dinner, he could tell instantly she was disappointed. They were still friendly, but at some point they would say that he wasn't what they'd expected. It had nothing to do with his size, of course not. Size didn't matter, it was all about those other 'inner qualities'. And they said it with a pitying look that he hated.

Strelitz lives in the Kreuzberg area of Berlin. He's the assistant manager of a supermarket. He pays a modest rent for his apartment, and always spends a week in the Tyrol at Christmas and two weeks in Tenerife during the summer. He's saved a bit of money, owns a four-year-old BMW, and belongs to a gym.

On the Saturday in question, Strelitz goes to the Turkish restaurant across from his apartment building, the same as he does nearly every evening. He orders grilled lamb, a salad and a beer. Then he takes his laptop from his briefcase and looks over the weekly order for the supermarket. The owner of the restaurant brings him his food and they have a brief chat. Strelitz closes his laptop. He eats slowly because he doesn't have anything else to do today. After he's finished his food, he drinks three glasses of raki – Turkish aniseed spirit.

At the next table are two men he's often seen at the restaurant before. One of them is very fat and has a black wolf tattooed on his neck. The other is tall and wears a woollen hat. They are talking quietly. The tall man uses his foot to push a sports bag under the table to the tattooed man. The tattooed man takes hold of it, gets up and leaves the restaurant. He crosses the narrow street and disappears into the entrance of Strelitz's apartment building. After a few minutes, he returns without the bag and sits back down at the table. The two men seem relaxed now. The tattooed man takes an electronic shisha pipe from his jacket and starts smoking. After a quarter of an hour, they pay the bill. Out on the street, they say their goodbyes and head off in different directions.

Strelitz has lived in Kreuzberg long enough to know what all this is about. The men are using his apartment building as a place to stash drugs – as what they call a 'bunker'. Strelitz orders another raki; he wants to have a quiet think. If he calls the police, they'll question him and his name will go on file. He's seen this happen often enough with shoplifting offences at the supermarket. It would be better just to wait. In a few days, the dealers will look for a new hiding place and the whole thing will sort itself out.

Strelitz finishes his drink and asks for the bill. He goes up to his apartment, sits on the sofa and turns on the TV. He can't concentrate on the film. He takes a torch and goes down to the basement. In one of the communal storage spaces, he finds the black bag under some planks, building debris and old paint cans. Strelitz opens it. Inside are five packages, each weighing about a kilo, thickly wrapped in cling film. They smell of petrol, vinegar and damp chalk. Strelitz returns them to the bag, and thinks long and hard. Then he leaves the building and goes back to the restaurant. He waits until he's the last customer there.

The owner of the restaurant comes over to his table and laughs. 'Still hungry?'

'No,' says Strelitz. He's known the man for a number of years.

'Would you like another drink? A glass of special raki, perhaps?'

'I'd like that.'

The owner fetches a bottle without a label and sits down with him. He fills two glasses to the brim.

'Homemade. Distilled by my mother.' He takes off his apron and hangs it over an empty chair.

'Thanks,' says Strelitz. They drink. The owner refills their glasses.

'How's work?'

'The usual.'

'And women?'

'Well . . .' Strelitz shrugs his shoulders. The owner laughs.

'Can I ask you something?' says Strelitz. The alcohol is warm in his stomach.

'What's that?'

'I remember a police raid here a few years ago. People said it had something to do with drugs.'

'They found nothing,' the owner says. He starts to get up.

'Please stay,' says Strelitz. 'That's not what this is about. It's just that you're the only one I can ask.'

'Ask what?'

'How much a kilo of cocaine costs.'

The owner of the restaurant raises his eyebrows. 'Depends on the quality. Between twenty and thirty.'

'Twenty thousand?' Strelitz is astonished.

'Yes. But why would you want a kilo of cocaine?'

'I don't.'

'Then why are you asking?'

'No reason.'

The owner fills their glasses again. They drink in silence.

'I want to sell it,' says Strelitz after a while.

'You have a kilo of cocaine?' The owner looks at him.

Strelitz nods. He's a little excited now.

'I can call someone,' says the owner eventually, and pours more raki.

'Who?'

'A friend.'

'And this friend, do you trust him?'

'Of course I trust him, he's a drug dealer.' The restaurant owner laughs, and this time Strelitz laughs with him. Two men having a private chat, thinks Strelitz, both with standing in the neighbourhood. He can feel the effects of the alcohol.

'And how much do you get?' asks Strelitz.

'Twenty per cent.' The owner suddenly turns serious.

'But it's not a game. If you start this, you have to finish it, too.'

He's switched to the familiar *du* form. Strelitz is one of them now; he feels proud.

'How long will it take your friend to get here?'

'I'll call him and he'll tell me when he can come. You bring the kilo here, and then we'll see how things go.'

'Sounds good.'

'You really have a kilo?'

'I have five,' says Strelitz.

'Five kilos?' The owner exhales loudly. 'I won't ask you where you got it, but if there's any trouble, it's your trouble, not mine. Are you sure you want to do this?'

Strelitz nods. The owner gets up, goes into an adjoining room and comes back with a small notebook. He puts on his reading glasses and taps a number into his mobile. He says a few sentences in Turkish, looks at Strelitz, carries on speaking, and then says: 'My friend can be here in ten minutes. Is that OK?'

'Yes,' says Strelitz.

'We'll meet in the kitchen. Use the back entrance. I'll go and lock up.'

Strelitz drains his glass. It's only when he stands up that he realises how drunk he is. He crosses the street, goes to his apartment, and gets the pepper spray he carries to protect himself from dogs when he goes jogging in the park. In the storage space, he sits on one of the planks and opens the bag again. It's all still there. He waits a couple of minutes and tries to sober up. Then he picks up the bag.

In front of the restaurant on the other side of the street, Strelitz sees the fat man with the wolf tattoo. The tattooed man stops. He stares at Strelitz. For a moment, neither man moves. Strelitz is the first to start running. His car is parked at the end of the street; it's about 500 metres away. The tattooed man lets out a roar. As he runs, Strelitz pulls the car key from his jacket and presses down on the fob. The BMW's locks pop up. Strelitz opens the door, throws the bag across to the passenger side and collapses into the driver's seat. The tattooed man is still yelling, his face red and sweaty. He reaches the car. Strelitz starts the engine and pulls down hard on the steering wheel. The tattooed man rips open the driver's door and reaches for Strelitz's neck. Strelitz blasts the pepper spray into his face and steps on the accelerator. The tattooed man is forced to let go. His forearm whacks against the door frame; he yelps with pain. The door slams shut.

Half of the pepper spray is still in the car. Strelitz's face burns, his skin swells, his eyes water. He coughs and splutters. In the rear-view mirror, he sees the tattooed man lying in the street, writhing and clutching his left foot. Then he can no longer see anything. The car slaloms, and grazes two parked cars. Strelitz keeps his foot on the accelerator, races onto the intersection, loses control, and collides head-on with one of the pillars supporting the elevated railway. The force of the impact lifts him out of his seat. His head hits the windscreen and he loses consciousness.

Seventeen hours later, he finds himself sitting before the examining judge in the district court. According to the judge, the sports bag contained 4.8 kilograms of almost pure cocaine. He'd also been in possession of a weapon, the pepper spray. She reads him the relevant laws, and says that he can expect a prison sentence of at least five years. If he wishes to say anything now, he can, but he is not obliged to do so.

Strelitz is wearing a buff-coloured cervical collar, his neck hurts, and his eyes are still bloodshot. He wants to think about it first, he says. The judge issues a warrant remanding him in custody for the drug offence.

Strelitz is taken to the detention facility. He's seen plenty of prison films: sadistic guards, food from tin bowls, prisoners raped in the showers or stabbed with homemade knives. But none of that happens. He gets a cell to himself. And then everything changes. For the first time in his life, people look at him with respect. The warrant is his badge of honour: 4.8 kilos of cocaine, the getaway in the car, the refusal to confess. Strelitz is no small-time dealer, but rather someone to be respected. Nobody makes fun of his size anymore, nobody uses words like 'dwarf', 'midget', or 'gnome', or says things like 'You'll understand when you grow up'. One of the prisoners knows Strelitz from the supermarket. He tells everyone that Strelitz only used his job as a cover for his drug dealing. Strelitz doesn't contradict him. When he's asked why he wasn't caught before, he smiles in a way that he hopes is enigmatic.

Six weeks before his trial, Strelitz is served with a penal order. It relates to his attempted escape, his drink driving and the accident. His blood alcohol content had measured 1.6. The punishment isn't particularly severe: a fine of thirty euros a day for ninety days, and disqualification from driving for a month. The court official tells Strelitz that he's entitled to lodge an appeal within two weeks if he so wishes. Strelitz grandly waves this aside. Given the drugs offence, it really doesn't matter, he says.

After spending four months in custody, his trial begins. Strelitz tells the police officer taking him to the courtroom that it's his first trial.

'It's usually quite dull,' says the police officer. 'Always the same thing.'

'It's already half eleven, but my summons was for nine o'clock,' says Strelitz.

'It happens. They often start late.'

'Are there many spectators?' asks Strelitz.

'No. I mean, it's not a big deal. There's a child murderer on trial in the other courtroom. Lots more action there.'

Strelitz is disappointed.

When he enters the courtroom, he sees that the judges, public prosecutor and defence counsel aren't wearing their robes. There are no spectators. The public prosecutor is sipping a bottle of water.

'Please take a seat, Mr Strelitz,' says the presiding judge. 'We're not proceeding with the case.'

Strelitz doesn't understand.

'Is it correct that you were served a penal order six weeks ago for driving under the influence of alcohol?' asks the judge.

Strelitz looks at his lawyer. She gives him a nod.

'Yes,' says Strelitz.

'And you didn't appeal?'

'No.' Strelitz thinks he's done something wrong.

'We only heard about this earlier today.'

'I'm sorry about that,' says Strelitz.

'Let me try to explain it to you,' says the presiding judge. 'You perhaps know that our laws forbid sentencing a person twice for the same crime.'

'Yes.'

'We lawyers call this *ne bis in idem* in Latin, which means "not twice in the same matter". It's a principle of fair criminal procedure that no one can be punished more than once for the same crime. In your case, it's like this: the district court has convicted you of driving under the influence using a penal order. Today is supposed to be the day that the drugs offence is heard.

That's two offences. But in actual fact it's not that simple. Because when we speak of an *offence* in court, we mean the conduct of the perpetrator in so far as it creates a so-called unified process. For example, if you steal a car and drive it to a bank that you then rob, we're talking about just one offence. In reality, the car theft and the bank robbery are two offences, but they can only be tried together. Do you understand?'

'I'm not sure,' says Strelitz.

'We're now of the view that the drink-driving offence and the drugs offence can't be separated from each other, precisely because the car was used to transport the narcotics. The two offences – the driving and the drugs offence – are thus legally only *one* offence. And as you've already been convicted for the driving offence, you can't be tried again.'

Strelitz stares at the judge.

'Have your lawyer explain it to you one more time. In any case, this trial can't take place, because our colleagues at the regional court have made a mistake. The proceedings will be discontinued in accordance with section 206a, paragraph 1, of the Code of Criminal Procedure. The custody order is revoked.'

The judges leave the courtroom. The defence lawyer puts her hand on Strelitz's shoulder. She's a head taller than him.

'What just happened?' asks Strelitz.

'You got lucky,' says the lawyer. 'Congratulations, you're free to go. They only convicted you of the *small* offence.'

The Diver

Good Friday

She knows the church so well – the wooden benches, the whitewashed walls, the high windows. This is where she made her First Communion; this is where she got married. She sits in the third row, the same seat as always. Her son is away, skiing with his grandparents since last week.

'This is the hour of the Lord's death,' says the priest.

It is the day of the Crucifixion. There are no candles today, no incense; the altar is bare, the triptych closed. The priest is wearing dark red vestments. She likes the unwavering ritual of the Mass. The kneeling, rising and praying never fail to calm her.

She thinks once again about her husband. They had met seventeen years earlier while working for the largest company in the region, a supplier for the automotive industry. At the time, she was part of the management's administrative team. He was from northern Germany, a boyish, lanky man. Even before meeting him, she fell in love with the photo on his job application. He looked so neat and clean-shaven, his hair parted. There were no omissions or spelling mistakes in his CV, the paper was spotless. She liked everything about it.

When he got the job, she congratulated him. They had lunch together a few times in the company canteen, and at some point he invited her to the cinema. That first evening he wore a new suede jacket with knitted cuffs. He smelled of soap and menthol, and she touched his white hands. Four days later they slept together.

His career flourished at the company – team leader, then chief engineer. Before the wedding, her father tried to warn her: the man wasn't from around here, the mountains and föhn wind could change a person. They married anyway and built a house in the country on land belonging to her parents' farm, with a view over meadows and fields, all the way to the Alps. As a child, she had gone to the village school; her first love had been the innkeeper's son, her best friend the baker's daughter. She was happy. Everything seemed to be going well.

'As a man, Christ took all of our sins upon Himself,' says the priest. The pharmacist is sitting in the pew in front of her. She counts the age spots on his balding head. A baby cries during the Intercession. She doesn't turn around, that wouldn't do. But she feels an inner warmth as she thinks of her own son.

The birth changed everything. Her husband had been with her in the delivery room at his own request. The doctor hadn't kept an eye on him. Later, she learned that he had watched her vagina opening, that he must have smelled her blood, urine and faeces. When the doctor laid the baby on her stomach, her husband remarked that its *vernix caseosa* looked like cheese spread. He kept coming back to that later.

When she arrived home with the newborn, he was caring and attentive. He did the shopping, cooking and cleaning, and brought the baby to her when it cried at night. Now, every evening at the front door, he would take off his shoes, wipe the soles clean, and place them on a cloth. He no longer carried coins in his trouser pockets; too many people had touched them, he said. Then things got worse. He kept waking up in the night, screaming and soaked with sweat. He had dreamed about his toenails, he said. They had been black, hugely enlarged, and were staring at him.

Sex became complicated. He didn't want to sleep with her in the bed anymore. He didn't want to dirty the sheets. The bathroom was the right place, the tiles were easy to clean. She went along with it for a while, but soon realised that he was having to force himself to touch her. One night she found him sitting on the bathroom floor by the radiator, masturbating with a rope around his neck while he watched porn on his mobile. She'd wanted to close the door again immediately, but he asked her to stay. After he came, he told her that this was the only way now. He kept seeing their son's head emerging from her body, his wet, black hair between her legs.

He grew withdrawn. When he came home from the factory, he would sit on the bench in front of the house. He sat there motionless for hours on end, his chin resting on his drawn-up knees, looking off into the mountains. When she tried to speak to him, he didn't reply. Only when they were lying in bed would he sometimes say something – bleak sentences she couldn't understand. He talked of deep-sea fish with no eyes, and planets of endless ice.

The first official warning from the company said that he had missed an important appointment, the second that he had locked himself in his office for a number of hours. At the butcher's, she heard the neighbours discussing her husband. And then the thing with the diving suit began.

After Mass, everyone stands for a while outside the church. She shakes hands with the priest. On the way home, she sees cowslip and wood anemones blossoming in the front gardens. It's a bright blue, windy spring day, and her hair blows into her face.

Half sitting, his buttocks a few centimetres off the floor, her husband is hanging from a rope tied to the bathroom's towel radiator. He's wearing the black diving suit he bought for their honeymoon in the Maldives. Small pieces of sliced cheese are pressed onto every inch of the suit; they stick to the rubber. Their plastic wrappers lie next to the body. Transparent cling film is wound around his head, rendering his face strangely smooth. His genitals hang from a hole in the diving suit. They look like an animal.

She spreads a towel over his genitals and sits on the edge of the bath. How much time elapses, she doesn't know. At some point she kneels next to the dead man. She lays his head in the crook of her arm, removes the cling film from his face and strokes his hair. She gathers up the cheese slices, some of which have already melted. It takes her almost two hours to undress him and heave him into the bed. She's exhausted and furious. She covers him, lies down by his side, and cries for nearly twenty minutes. Then she falls asleep.

When she wakes up, she feels lucid and true. She takes a long, hot shower, and puts on some fresh clothes and make-up. She phones the family doctor from the living room.

The doctor sees the subconjunctival punctiform haemorrhages in the deceased man's eyes and the injury to the neck. He'll have to call the police, he tells her. This wasn't a natural death. They wait in the kitchen until the police arrive from the district's largest town. It's already after midnight.

At the police station, they remove her belt and shoelaces. Suicide risk, the duty officer says. She has to put her house keys, watch, necklace, wedding ring and handbag in a red plastic box. She is searched.

During the questioning, she keeps saying that she found her husband in bed. The officer is young, and is on duty over the holiday weekend because he's not yet married and doesn't have children. He says that she strangled her husband in bed, while he was asleep, then showered and called the family doctor. The towels in the bathroom were still damp. There was no point denying it any longer; she should just tell him why she did it. When she refuses to say more, she's taken back to her cell.

Easter Saturday

The police station is a washed concrete building from the 1960s. She's taken to see a lawyer in a conference room. All the tables, chairs and computers are covered in plastic, and it smells of paint and varnish. She says she needs to shower. The policeman apologises and tells her that won't be possible, as the entire building is currently being redecorated. He removes her handcuffs.

Once she's alone with the lawyer, she repeats what she said to the policeman. The lawyer listens. He turns a fountain pen between his fingers and looks at her. It's often better, he says, if a defence lawyer doesn't know the truth. That makes it easier to ask questions, to find holes in the indictment, anything partial or illogical. But this is different, he says. There's already too strong a case against her. She would be placed on remand, and even if the defence managed to get her off in a few months' time, her life in the village would have been destroyed.

She looks silently out the window. She thinks about how the Easter fires will be lit on Monday to mark the end of the darkest time of year. With flattened hands, she strokes the plastic covering the table until there are no more wrinkles left. Suddenly she starts talking very fast. She tells the lawyer about her marriage, her husband and her son. 'He wasn't normal anymore,' she says. She doesn't know why, perhaps it was the föhn wind coming down from the mountains. She describes how she really found him. The village must never know, she says. She still has to live there, after all. That was the only reason why she'd moved him to the bed: she wanted to protect him and herself from the scandal, otherwise it would never go away. The lawyer doesn't interrupt. 'What on earth was wrong with him?' she asks, and starts to cry. The lawyer looks up. 'People do things like that,' he says. He gives her a tissue. As she was only arrested today, the warrant to remand her in custody would be issued tomorrow. He would speak to the judge.

Later, an officer brings sandwiches, a yoghurt and some drinks to her cell; no hot food, as unfortunately the canteen is also closed. He leans over. He shouldn't really tell her this, but the homicide unit has found the black plastic bag containing the diving suit in her garage. Everyone is waiting on the forensic pathologist's report.

She doesn't touch her food. That night, she hardly sleeps either.

Easter Sunday

She sits on a wooden bench outside the judge's chambers. The lawyer speaks to her in quiet tones. He says that when a man is aroused, a gland behind the bladder is stimulated long before he ejaculates. It produces a secretion, and tiny amounts of sperm leak out with this liquid. The forensic pathologist found such traces on the diving suit. She finds it hard to listen; the words discomfort her. The rope they found matches the marks on his neck, the lawyer says. The cheese, plastic wrappers and cling film all have the dead man's fingerprints on them. That exonerates her. Nonetheless, the public prosecutor has requested that a warrant be issued to remand her in custody. Murders are rare here, and she would like the examining judge to make a ruling.

The judge is wearing a corduroy jacket and checked shirt. He doesn't look like a judge is supposed to look, she thinks. She imagines his life when he's not at court: how he eats his lunch, takes his children to school, watches TV in the evenings. The judge asks her if she wants to make a statement and she shakes her head. The lawyer tells the whole story again. She listens, but it all sounds far away, unreal, her husband a stranger. She wants to go home, but doesn't know where.

The judge calls the forensic pathologist into the room. He is sworn in as an expert witness. He states that the cause of death is clear: the rope constricted the man's carotid arteries and he suffocated. Why people did this to themselves was not yet fully understood, but it had long been known that a lack of oxygen to the brain intensified orgasms. This was probably due to the limbic system, possibly also the medulla. Such practices had been documented for centuries. Even the Greeks were aware of them, and some antique Roman vases depicted strangulation as a means of heightening pleasure.

'He'd probably done it many times before. We found some older injuries on his larynx,' says the forensic pathologist.

'What was the cling film for?' asks the judge.

'Some kind of fetish; the smell of cheese, plastic and rubber probably aroused him. In any case, we can rule out the cling film as a cause of death. We found some holes in it that allowed him to breathe. Their edges showed traces of the deceased's saliva.'

'Aren't things like the cheese slices and the diving suit odd?'

'These sorts of incidents happen all the time. A few months ago, we found a man in a plastic bin bag. He had put on women's underwear, tied his legs together and fastened the opening over his head. Then he'd used a vacuum cleaner to suck the air out of the bag, activating it via a toggle switch on a cable inside the bag. It was a really complicated set-up. The man made just one mistake: the vacuum cleaner was too powerful. After a few seconds there was no air left in the bag, and the plastic was pulled so tightly against his body that he couldn't reach the switch. The vacuum cleaner kept running and the man suffocated.'

The judge nods. 'And what exactly happened in our case – at least as far as you can tell?'

'The man tied a rope to the radiator, placed it around his neck, then let himself slide slowly down while he was masturbating. The noose tightened. Only a small amount of pressure is needed to occlude the carotid arteries.'

'Is it a painful death?'

'No. It happens very quickly; there's no time to feel a sense of suffocation. The total closure of the carotid arteries results in a loss of consciousness after roughly fifteen seconds. If compression is maintained, brain death occurs in about ten to twelve minutes.'

'You say that he'd probably done this a number of times before, so what do you think went wrong this time?'

'There are a few possibilities. If he was hanging too long from the radiator, he may simply not have had the strength to free himself. Perhaps he tried, but slipped – his feet could have gone out from under him on the bathroom tiles. Or perhaps he passed out too quickly. This type of auto-erotic stimulation is always extremely dangerous, but many still do it because they experience themselves more intensely that way. People who favour these sexual practices say that they don't just have an orgasm – they *are* the orgasm. They do it repeatedly. It's like an addiction.'

'If I understand you correctly, there's no evidence of external interference,' says the lawyer.

'I can't completely rule out that another person was involved in his death. But at the same time, there's absolutely no evidence to indicate that this was the case. So yes, from a forensic point of view, we have to assume it was an accident.'

They all look at each other briefly. The lawyer writes something in his notebook and the judge dictates a summary to the clerk.

'If there are no further questions . . .' says the judge, looking at the public prosecutor and the defence lawyer. Both shake their heads. 'Then I will allow the expert witness to step down. Thank you very much for your time today. I wish you a Happy Easter.'

The forensic pathologist gathers his papers and leaves the room. The public prosecutor says that she's withdrawing her request for a warrant to remand the woman in custody. The judge nods. He pulls a green slip of paper from his desk drawer and signs it.

Then he tells her she is free.

Easter Monday

The altar cloths are back in place, the triptych is open, the body of Jesus Christ is lying in Mary's lap. Before the service, in the churchyard, members of the congregation offered her their sympathies on the death of her husband. Later, the neighbours will call round for afternoon coffee. The funeral is in two weeks' time. She will choose the readings with the priest; the lesson will be dignified and sombre. No one has any idea she was detained, and no one will find out, the lawyer has promised her that. This morning, she stood in front of the radiator in the bathroom. *He's not here*, she thought.

The Mass is joyful, and the church seems brighter than usual to her. 'By grace you have been saved,' says the priest. Then he blesses the congregation, and everyone stands and starts to sing. She's known this hymn since she was a child. In that moment, she decides to forgive herself. All she did was press his head against the rope until he grew very calm, his slender white hands lying peacefully on the floor. Today is the Day of Redemption. 'Kyrie eleison', that's all she wants to think of now. Then she joins in the singing of the Easter Monday Resurrection hymn.

Stinky Fish

In his part of the city, parents didn't take their kids to school. It was different a few kilometres to the west. Tom had seen it once. There, parents pulled school bags from cars, kissed their children and walked them to the school gates. The parents all looked identical and the children looked identical, too.

But here, in his neighbourhood, there were people from 160 countries. The rules were different and childhoods were shorter.

They met up in front of the bakery, like every morning. Tom's friend was telling a story about a girl. It wasn't so easy, he said, you could get lots of things wrong, and then girls would run off and say stupid things about you. Tom nodded, but wasn't paying much attention. He was supposed to have stolen some cigarettes from the supermarket while the others waited outside. He hadn't been able to do it.

They walked the same route as always, Tom and his friend and the others. They were discussing the dare, and were serious and quiet. Tom was scared.

They called the man Stinky Fish. Usually, they crossed to the other side of the street when they reached his house. He always sat on a raffia chair under the little porch roof. He sat there even when it rained or snowed. During the war, a bomb had destroyed the front and side portions of the house – only the rear of the building remained. Weeds grew out the front; there were car tyres lying around, mildewed planks, a pick-axe without a handle, a broken fuse box. The walls of the house were mouldy, the cellar windows broken. And then there was the smell of fishmeal, burnt milk and petrol. On hot days it stank all the way to the school. There were lots of stories about Stinky Fish. He was wanted for murder in almost every nation, they said. He had been seen angling in the river and biting the heads off live fish; he warmed milk for the city rats in his cellar. Some said that he had a key to the school, and that he walked the corridors at night and licked the students' metal lockers.

The whole way over, Tom hoped that Stinky Fish wouldn't be at home. But there he was, as always.

Stinky Fish wore black sunglasses, his jacket had holes, his trousers were dirty. But his shoes were shiny. They looked like really good shoes. They didn't go with the rest of the man and they didn't go with the smell.

They came to a halt in front of the property. Tom tried to bargain. 'I'll give the cigarettes another try. I'll get whole cartons. This time I'll do it.' He had said these sentences over and over in his head, but now they didn't sound as good as he'd thought they would. The others were having none of it. 'Too late,' they said. Now he had to go and see Stinky Fish. He had to take at least five paces beyond the fence, and then stop and shout 'Stinky Fish'. Or else he was a coward and everyone would get to call him that from now on.

Tom gave his school bag to the others. *They'll give my stuff to my mum if Stinky Fish kills me*, he thought. He went through the open garden gate and counted off the paces towards the house. He stopped at exactly five. Stinky Fish hadn't moved at all yet. Tom could hardly bear the stench. The moss on the stone slabs was damp, even though it was really warm.

He took a breath, shut his eyes and shouted, 'Hello, Stinky Fish.' He realised straight away how stupid it was. He wanted to add something else, something friendly, but he couldn't think of what to say. His head was empty, his mouth dry.

The man raised his head. Tom could see himself in the lenses of the sunglasses. There were beads of sweat on the man's bald cranium. The man took off the glasses. Tom saw the movement and wanted to run away, but couldn't. Stinky Fish was blind: his left eye was white and dead. But the other eye was staring at Tom. The edges of the pupil were ragged, blue fragments floated in the iris. The eye got bigger and bigger. Sounds and colours and even the stench vanished into the eye; it absorbed everything. Tom felt dizzy. He shook. Then suddenly he saw Antarctica before him, images from the world atlas in school: snowfields, glaciers, frozen waterfalls. He had no idea how much time passed. Finally, Stinky Fish put his glasses back on and lowered his head. Tom's arms and legs ached. And then he saw it. An open bar of chocolate lay on the blind man's knees. It was the same chocolate that his mother bought at the greengrocer's on the high street. And although he was only eleven, in that moment he understood: there was no mystery, the old man wasn't a murderer, he didn't bite the heads off live fish. He was just a blind old man with a bar of chocolate.

Tom went up to him. It was easy now.

'That was stupid of me,' he said softly.

'Yes,' said the blind man.

'I'm sorry.' Tom waited, but the blind man didn't respond.

'I'm going to go now,' he said after a while.

The blind man nodded.

Tom turned around. Suddenly he heard his friends yelling. The first stone flew past him. Tom couldn't see who had thrown it. The stone hit the old man on the head; his dark glasses hung from one ear, the lenses were shattered. The man held his hands in front of his face. Blood was seeping through his fingers. The stones were hitting him all over.

The police came to the classroom in the very first lesson. A neighbour had seen the children running off towards the school. He had described their clothing – one of them, who didn't have a school bag, had gone up to the old man.

At the police station, the policewoman kept asking Tom why they had done it. She showed him photos from the hospital: gauze bandages were wrapped around the blind man's head. Tom said nothing, because no one in their neighbourhood talked to the police. After half an hour the policewoman gave up. In her report, she identified Tom as the 'suspected ringleader'. His mother came to pick him up.

No charges were brought against the children; they were too young. The only people who spoke with the parents were social workers. They wrote up reports on housing conditions and family circumstances, and opened case files. The teacher reprimanded the pupils. The day before the start of the summer holidays, an elderly police officer in uniform visited the class and gave a talk about violent juvenile crime. He handed out leaflets, which then lay scattered all over the playground and street.

A few months later the old man's house was torn down, and a shopping centre and car park were built in its place. The name Stinky Fish lived on in the children's memories for a while, then it faded and vanished completely.

The Lake House

Felix Ascher is born with tiny red dots on his stomach. His parents think it's an allergy. Babies sometimes get this sort of thing, their friends say: washing detergent or milk could be to blame, it'll clear up of its own accord. But the marks don't go away. The capillaries under the skin dilate and fill with blood. They flow into one another, and eighteen weeks later almost his entire upper body, his neck and the right-hand side of his face are coloured a light red. They are port-wine stains, a small genetic defect.

Felix's mother is thirty-nine years old and his father is forty-three. For both, it is their second marriage. They have jobs with municipal utility companies in Munich. His father is a supply engineer, his mother works in accounting. Felix is their only child.

At the age of four he visits his grandfather for the first time. The grandfather was born in Shanghai at the end of the 1920s; his parents were doctors at the

German Medical School there. Later, he lived in Hong Kong and made a fortune importing industrial equipment from Germany. When his wife died, he moved to Germany and bought a house in Upper Bavaria, about sixty kilometres south of Munich. The house, a seventeenth-century dairy, was once part of a monastery, and has always been called the Lake House. It lies just beyond a small village, slightly elevated on a hill – a plain, square building with thick walls and nineteen rooms. From there, you can see far across the lake, and in föhn weather the landscape turns a deep, dark blue all the way to the Alps. A hundred years ago, Wassily Kandinsky, Franz Marc, Paul Klee and Lovis Corinth painted in this region. Later, Ödön von Horváth and Bertolt Brecht lived here, and Thomas Mann's *Doctor Faustus* is set in a nearby village.

In the grandfather's house, the curtains are always half drawn, the light is soft and subdued, the rooms are quiet. There is dark, hardwood flooring, and the walls are covered in a pale yellow chinoiserie wallpaper of landscapes with mandarin trees, cherry and apple blossom, cranes, dragonflies and exotic birds. The furniture dates from the 1920s and 1930s, and is from the British Ambassador's residence in Shanghai.

There is no television or radio, just a record player made of wood. The library contains two worn leather armchairs, a sagging sofa with a light green linen cover, smoking and card tables, and a bamboo newspaper rack. The grandfather often sits there and reads. He wears a white three-piece linen suit and smokes oval cigarettes he has imported from Egypt. Felix plays at his feet on a faded silk carpet, whose pattern serves as a labyrinth for his toy figurines.

The grandfather has rooms on the second floor made up for Felix. He's given a toy train with a black locomotive made of iron, and two dark green wagons, through whose windows he can see passengers. Every evening, the grandfather switches on the magic lantern by his bed. It projects silhouettes onto the wall, scenes from Shanghai: ships being unloaded, Chinese people smoking long pipes, a dog wearing a bow on its head and running through the streets.

As Felix grows older, he starts to feel ashamed of the marks on his skin. The other children pick on him. His parents take him to see a succession of doctors. Time and again, he is made to undress: he's examined, irradiated, given ointments and injections, but the marks don't change. Only the grandfather is different. He tells of people in China who have a third nipple or a sixth finger, and who are worshipped because the gods have singled them out to lead special lives. The marks are actually a secret map. Felix need only look carefully, and then he'll be able to read them too. The mark above his belly button is the land of mythical creatures, where dragons, mermaids and invincible heroes live. And there, on his chest, that's the land of wise men, where the cleverest people gather to discuss world affairs. But that small mark on his cheek, which looks a bit like the lake in front of the house, is the most important of them all, because that's where happiness has made its home.

The grandfather takes a daily walk from the house to the village. In the summer, he wears a hat of woven straw. The villagers greet him politely; everyone knows him, of course. *By his side*, thinks Felix, *it's safe*. They always sit on the same bench by the lake. The grandfather closes his eyes, takes Felix's hand in his own, and has the boy describe what he sees: a dried bird's nest, a rowing boat with a snapped oar, cart tracks in the grass. Then the grandfather tells Felix of his childhood in Shanghai, of the midday heat and amber afternoon light, of the rain, the evening gowns worn by beautiful women and the hotels with French names, of water towns, cockfights and opium addicts. And gradually, the visual and spoken images conflate in the boy's mind: the rape fields, clover meadows and reeds on the lake shore merge with the street smells of Shanghai, the cries of the market traders, and the emerald green palms. And it is only here, in front of the Lake House, only in the quiet of this gentle landscape in the Alpine foothills, that he feels calm.

Felix Ascher is fourteen when his grandfather dies. Thereafter, his life proceeds uneventfully – 'law-abiding' and 'problem-free', as the judge will say much later. Secondary school, military service, university. At twenty-six, he takes a job with an insurance company in Hamburg. At thirty-five, he's made deputy head of the claims department. At forty-two, he's put in charge of the Northern Region, and at forty-six, he secures a transfer to Istanbul. Three years later, he's divisional director of the Arab Region. He works long hours. He visits prostitutes because he doesn't want to impose his looks on anybody. Once, at an insurance company seminar, Ascher is asked to name his life goal. He's able to answer without hesitation: he wants to move back to the Lake House someday. He keeps a picture of his grandfather on the bedside table in his apartment.

Ascher is fifty-four when his mother dies; his father had died twelve years earlier. He goes back to Germany for the funeral. 'In the midst of life we are in death,' the pastor says. This sentence sticks in Ascher's mind.

On the return journey to Istanbul he starts to feel unsettled. Increasingly, he loses interest in his work; he gets sloppy and finds it hard to concentrate. At night, he keeps thinking that he's wasted his life.

After two months, he discusses his financial situation with his tax advisor. The capital he inherited from his mother, his parents' apartment, and a severance package from the company would give him enough for a comfortable life. He thinks on it for another two months, then applies to take early retirement. He dismantles his household in Istanbul and sells his parents' apartment in Munich. Six months after his mother's funeral, Ascher is a free man. He moves into the Lake House.

His parents had moved his grandfather's old furniture and books up to the attic, stripped the faded wallpaper, laid carpets and whitewashed the rooms. They rarely stayed at the Lake House – just occasional weekends and short breaks.

Ascher has the furniture brought back downstairs. A carpenter from the village repairs the wooden blinds and shelves, restores the tables and the bureau, and sands the floorboards. Ascher spends weeks searching the internet for wallpaper. He eventually finds a retailer in London, who sells him some rolls from the 1920s that match the original chinoiserie wallpaper. He has the leather armchairs and the linen sofa cleaned. He even has the wooden record player reconditioned by a workshop in Munich.

In the space of a year, with the exception of a few modern conveniences, he's restored the house to how it looked during his grandfather's time.

He spends the following years at the Lake House and in the village. He seldom travels. In the summer, he breakfasts every morning at the bakery; in the evenings he goes to the village inn on the market square or to the ice-cream parlour. He forges good relations with the villagers, makes donations to the volunteer fire brigade, and attends village events, the Corpus Christi procession and folk festivals. Ascher is viewed by everyone as friendly and pleasant. He has, as they say in the village, *fitted right in.*

Occasionally, he still goes to the theatre or the cinema in Munich. When he drives back up the unmade road to the Lake House, he stays sitting in the car for a few minutes before getting out. He turns off the headlights and waits until everything around him is quiet once more.

Five years after Ascher's return, the decision is taken at a village meeting to sell the abandoned fishermen's houses by the lake to an investor. They're owned by the local council and have been standing empty for years. The investor receives planning permission to demolish the single-storey buildings and to build five modest holiday homes within the boundaries of the plot. The village hopes to stimulate tourism and an upswing in retail and gastronomy.

The plot of land is situated on the shores of the lake, only a short distance from Ascher's house. When he hears about the plans, he's horrified. He speaks to the mayor, tries to talk round individual council members, and tells everyone that it's absolutely essential to leave everything as it is. This has no effect. Ascher hires a lawyer, brings lawsuits, and loses. No one in the village can understand why he's so worked up. From then on, Ascher does his shopping in the neighbouring town. Only the cleaning lady and a drinks supplier are allowed to enter the Lake House.

He monitors the construction work, which begins in the spring, from the bench in front of the Lake House. If his driveway is blocked for more than half an hour, or if the work starts before seven in the morning, he calls the police. To begin with, the young policewoman from the village comes out to see him, but she soon realises that he's just a troublemaker and stops responding to his calls.

The holiday homes go up quickly, small wooden bungalows with three rooms apiece. The external walls are painted red, blue and green. Within three months all have been sold. Young families with children spend their holidays and weekends here.

Ascher changes. His cleaning lady hears him talking to himself, ranting for hours at a time. He lets himself go. He eats hardly anything, stops going to the barber's and sleeps in his clothes. Sometimes he stays in bed for days. He buys himself a pair of binoculars and keeps a log: who holds parties outside their holiday homes after 11.00 p.m., who fails to sort their recycling properly, who mows the lawn on Sundays, whose children shriek in the quiet of the afternoon. He sends his notes to the police, the regional council, and the state premier. Although his complaints are sometimes valid, they are ignored.

One Sunday evening in late summer, Ascher can't take any more. It's been noisy the whole weekend. *Lakeside Summer Festival*, they called it – they'd even put an invitation through his door. For three days, the entire shoreline had been packed with cars bearing Munich licence plates. They had set up great big speakers on the beach, built a huge fire, and then danced, shouted and laughed loudly.

Every day that summer, Ascher had imagined how he would go about it. Down in the cellar is his grandfather's gun cabinet, containing two rusty pistols, three rifles and eight packs of ammunition. The weapons are unregistered; his grandfather had shipped them over at some point in a container from China.

Ascher takes one of the rifles from the rack, a Swiss Army carbine from the Second World War. He still remembers how to handle it from his military service days. He takes the rifle apart, cleans and oils the parts, fills the magazine and loads it. He aims it at the door. Over and over he says out loud to himself: 'Enough is enough,' and 'It's time to put a stop to this.'

He sits on the bench in front of the house with a bottle of schnapps and gets slowly drunk. The rifle leans next to him against the wall. When it's suitably dark, he pulls on the pink washing-up gloves he found in the kitchen. Ascher has worked for long enough in the claims department of an insurance company to know the mistakes that perpetrators make. He walks down the path to the lake. The lights are on in just one of the houses; the other families have long since driven back to the city.

Ascher kicks at the wooden door with his boot. The house is owned by a hotel manager and his family: two children, one dog. The woman opens the door wearing a bathrobe. She is twenty-nine years old. When she sees the muzzle of the rifle, she screams and turns to the side – a reflex. The bullet enters her body under the armpit, penetrating both of her lungs and her heart. She falls to the floor. Ascher steps over her and looks in the other rooms. Her husband has already returned to Munich with the two children. She'd wanted to stay on a bit to tidy things up.

In spite of her injuries, she manages to crawl to the doorstep. Ascher positions himself so that he's standing over her and reloads the rifle. 'Once you've started something . . .' he says. The projectile severs her spinal column between the fifth and sixth neck verte-brae. He drags the corpse back into the house by its feet, turns off the lights, exits and closes the door.

In the cellar of the Lake House, he uses an angle grinder to cut the rifle into three on the workbench. Then he strips naked and stuffs his clothes, the wash-ing-up gloves and his shoes into a bin bag. He showers and puts on fresh clothing. He drives a few kilometres to the Murnauer Moos, a vast area of marshland. He throws the three rifle pieces and the ammunition into separate holes in the mire. He burns the clothes.

The body is only discovered on Wednesday. The husband hadn't been able to reach his wife and had gone to the house. At first, the officers from the near-est town's homicide unit suspect the husband, then they think it was a robbery, and finally they're at a loss. They check whether the family has any enemies, but that doesn't lead anywhere either. The owners of the other holiday homes are called in for question-ing – all of them have an alibi. Ascher is questioned too; he tells them he saw and heard nothing. Only the young village policewoman remembers that he took legal action to block the construction of the holiday homes and frequently made complaints. The public prosecutor applies for a warrant to search Ascher's house, but the application is rejected by the examining judge. 'That's a very weak theory,' he says.

One night, five days after the crime, Ascher slips on the cellar steps while drunk, breaking his hip and hitting his head on the stone steps. He lies there unconscious for around thirty minutes. When he comes to, he can't move. He's only found the next morning by the cleaning lady, who immediately calls the emergency services on her mobile. The young policewoman drives over to the Lake House and watches Ascher being taken off to hospital by an ambulance. She's alone in the cellar for a few minutes. The doors of the gun cabinet are ajar, so she opens them. Its interior is lined with green velvet. There are rifles in two of the holders; the third is empty, but the indentation of a rifle butt is still visible in the velvet. She reports it to the homicide unit.

This time the public prosecutor is successful. While Ascher is in hospital, forensics officers search his house. The two rifles are ruled out as murder weapons; the ammunition doesn't match the projectiles that killed the woman either. Ascher's cleaning lady is questioned. The cabinet was always kept locked, she says. The police treat this as circumstantial evidence. Had Ascher changed at all, the cleaning lady is asked? 'He's always talking to himself and often drinks too much, but he's never done me any harm,' she says.

The police are convinced that Ascher had something to do with the murder, but can't get any further. Finally, the public prosecutor applies to have covert listening devices planted in Ascher's hospital room. The investigators hope that he'll say something about the murder to his visitors. The judge hesitates, then allows it. A policeman installs microphones in the room while Ascher is having hip surgery.

Over the next few days, the police listen to Ascher's monologues: he complains about his broken hip, about his headaches, about the poor food, the stupid nurses, the incompetent doctors. But nobody visits him. One night, when the investigators are about to give up, he suddenly starts talking about the murder. He says: 'I should have done it long ago,' and, 'Now I'll finally have some peace,' and, 'I should have burned them down right away, those bastards.' He is the only person in the hospital room.

Ascher is immediately arrested. During the police interview, he is played the tape. 'This is a confession,' they say to him. Where are the weapon and the ammunition, they want to know? He should just admit everything; things would go better for him that way; he couldn't get out of it now, in any case. Ascher keeps saying that he's innocent. He only asks for a lawyer after five hours of questioning. The judge orders that he be held in custody on a charge of murder.

In prison, Ascher goes to confession. He tells the priest that he no longer understands himself; he doesn't understand what he's done. 'I'm a bad person,' he says.

Four weeks after Ascher's arrest, a hearing to review the custody order takes place before the examining judge. The judge informs him that he is not obliged to say anything, then talks at length to Ascher's lawyer and the public prosecutor. They discuss the right to remain silent, as well as diaries, surveillance measures, and rulings by the highest courts.

Ascher tries to picture the young woman he shot. What was the colour of her hair? Had she said anything? Her toenails were painted red, he still remembers that. Suddenly he is filled with fear, a vague, nebulous fear – of what he is unsure. He stands up. The lawyer quietly tells him to sit down again. But Ascher stays on his feet. He has to say something now.

'I . . .' His mouth is dry, he's unable to move. *How I'd love to be at the Lake House now*, he thinks. *It used to be so simple there. And peaceful.*

'Yes?' says the judge. He says it in a friendly way.

'I . . . I . . .' Ascher feels sick; his hip is hurting him again. He hopes that his lawyer will say something, but nobody says anything. The judge looks at him. Ascher looks at the floor. He doesn't know what to do. Then he sits back down.

The judge takes off his reading glasses and puts them on the table in front of him. 'Mr Ascher, what is it you wish to tell us?'

'Nothing. I'm sorry.'

'Did anyone visit you in hospital?' asks the judge.

'My client has indicated that he wishes to remain silent,' says the lawyer very loudly.

'No, nobody,' replies Ascher.

'Do you sometimes talk to yourself?' asks the judge.

'Yes.'

'In hospital, too?'

'I think so,' says Ascher.

'Yes,' says the judge, and nods. He puts his glasses back on and writes something on his notepad. The lawyer talks some more. *She has an unpleasant voice*, thinks Ascher. The public prosecutor keeps interrupting her. Their exchanges become heated. She has brought some documents with her, and pushes them across the table to the judge. They are court rulings, Ascher gets that much. After half an hour, the judge says that he's heard all the arguments; he needs to consider them now; the hearing to review the custody order will pause for the day.

The following morning, Ascher is brought back to the judge's chambers. His lawyer is wearing her hair up today. Ascher thinks of the young woman's neck. She had been wearing a green bathrobe that smelled freshly washed, he'd noticed that straight away. She had white underwear on beneath, but he only saw that when there was blood everywhere. He takes his seat.

'A person's thoughts may not be monitored,' says the examining judge. 'Unlike when we keep diaries, talking to ourselves means speaking our thoughts, and these should never be accessible to others or recorded. They belong to a person's private sphere. The constitutional state distinguishes itself from the unconstitutional state thus: it may not determine the truth at any price. It sets limits on itself. We all know how hard it is to put up with these limits sometimes. But we cannot make use of the recordings from the hospital, because a person's thoughts must be free. They must never be subject to investigation by the state. And as there is no other evidence in the present case that suggests the accused should be regarded as a prime suspect, the court hereby revokes the custody order. The weapons violation – merely being in possession of the rifles and pistols – does not justify further detention.'

The public prosecutor is furious. He lodges an immediate appeal against the ruling and asks that Ascher continue to be held in custody until a decision is reached.

'No,' says the judge. He is very calm, and closes the red file lying on the table in front of him, which bears Ascher's name. 'My decision is made in accordance with the settled case law of the Federal Court of Justice. I don't believe that a higher court would rule otherwise. I deny your request.'

Two hours later, Ascher leaves the detention centre through a side door; journalists are waiting outside the main entrance. He has arranged to meet his lawyer at a bus stop.

'You shouldn't go back to the village for the time being,' says the lawyer. 'Wait until everything calms down.' She takes him to a B&B near the courts. He's given a small room on the first floor. Ascher puts down his bag and turns on the TV. The case is being reported on the regional news – he sees pictures of the village, the holiday homes and the Lake House. Ascher lies down on the bed. He unbuttons his shirt and runs his fingers over the marks on his skin.

Around midnight, he gets up and sits on the balcony. People are coming out of the cinema across the street after the last film showing. They'll spend some time with their friends now, thinks Ascher. They'll talk about the film and about their work and about other things. And then they'll go home to their houses and apartments.

Six years later, Ascher dies of liver cancer in a clinic. He never did return to the village. He tried several times to sell the house, which was now referred to locally as 'the murder house'. A distant relative, whom Ascher met just once when she was a little girl, is his sole heir. She lives in Madrid, has no need of the house, and gifts it to the village. The upper two floors become a local history museum; the ground floor is leased to a chef, who opens a restaurant there. According to its website, the terrace 'offers a chance to enjoy the peace of the lake and views across the Blue Land'.

Subbotnik

Seyma's father came to Germany from Turkey at the age of eighteen and soon found work at a coal mine in the Ruhr. At nineteen, he married a girl from his homeland, a union arranged by his parents. At twenty, he became a father for the first time. He knew very little about the country where he worked and whose language he did not speak. *One day*, he would go back. Noah's Ark had come to rest above his village on Mount Ararat, he liked to say. He put aside money to build a family home there, and kept the plans on the top shelf of the living-room cupboard.

Seyma was his eldest daughter. But she wasn't like the girls back home. She didn't want to wear a head-scarf, he had to force her. She took no interest in her parents' traditions or religion. Even at a young age, she felt there must be something beyond the block of flats where they lived. She wanted more, much more. Seyma's father was stricter with her than with her sisters. He was afraid for her and that made him want to break her. As often as not, she was grounded; her pocket money was repeatedly withheld; she had to clean the flat and wash his car. But she was tough and rode it out. At sixteen she transferred to a secondary school with a strong academic record. The day after receiving her final exam results, she announced that she was leaving home to study in another city. Her father began shouting at her. If she left now, he would disown her. He tried to hit her, but Seyma's mother stepped between them. When Seyma left for the station the next day, her mother secretly left the flat as well. On the train, she embraced her daughter and gave her all the money she had. 'It'll be OK, he'll calm down soon,' her mother said, but Seyma knew that wasn't true.

For eight weeks, she lived with an uncle in Berlin and helped out at his restaurant. Then she was accepted to study Law and moved into student accommodation. She spent the next two years making up for lost time. She drank alcohol, took ecstasy and cocaine, and went clubbing until the early hours of the morning. She wasn't interested in lectures; she wanted a different kind of life. Sometimes she would call her mother and speak to her for a couple of minutes, without ever talking about herself. It was only after waking up naked between two strangers following a party, without a clue where she was, that she got frightened. She didn't want to fail her parents or herself. She began to study hard.

On days when she had no lectures, she would visit the criminal courts to observe trials. On one occasion, she watched an older lawyer whose client was charged with tax evasion. In the course of a search, a packet of Viagra and a strap-on dildo had been found in the defendant's safe. When a policeman made fun of this during the trial, the old lawyer looked up from his files. 'Do you think it right to mock the weaknesses of others?' he asked. It was only a single sentence, delivered in a quiet, almost flat way, which had nothing to do with the trial or the defendant's guilt. But afterwards there was silence in the courtroom and Seyma thought about her own life. Five years later, she applied for a job with the same lawyer.

The law firm had a good reputation. The senior partner, the one Seyma had seen at trial, had become famous forty years earlier for his tough stance in court – a 'combative defence' they'd called it back then. These days, the firm's lawyers focused almost exclusively on corporate criminal law. They spent their days at their desks, charging between 600 and 1,000 euros an hour. Going to trial was the exception – most matters were settled out of court with lengthy legal agreements. The firm only took on cases involving serious criminality once or twice a year. It's just part and parcel of what we do, said the senior partner, whom everybody called the Old Man. In his view, one could only understand the Code of Criminal Procedure by spending time in court; only there did it come alive.

Seyma wasn't nervous about the interview. She had passed two state examinations with distinction, worked as a research associate with a Professor of Criminal Law, and had written fourteen commentaries on judgements for legal journals. Her dissertation explored European Court of Human Rights case law in relation to the issue of pre-trial detention. She had come a long way.

The law firm's office manager led her into a large meeting room. He was balding, with pale pink skin and protruding incisors. She enquired after the senior partner, but the office manager explained that he didn't involve himself in the firm's administrative affairs. This included the recruitment of lawyers, secretaries, trainees and interns.

The office manager went through everything with her: work placements, exam results, evaluations by judges and public prosecutors, her dissertation, her personal interests. He did his job well. He asked questions designed to put Seyma under pressure: 'Name one thing you would never exchange for money'; 'What question would you rather not be asked?'; 'What's the biggest mistake you've ever made?' She answered everything in a calm and friendly manner. It all seemed rather silly to her, but she didn't let it show. The office manager rarely looked at her face – he mostly stared at her breasts. Seyma had met his type before.

After twenty minutes, the Old Man joined them after all.

'Don't let me disturb you,' he said, crossing the room. He sat down at the end of the table. 'Who put those flowers there?' he asked.

'The new secretary,' said the office manager.

'Why?' asked the Old Man.

'Because it creates a friendlier—'

'I want them out,' interjected the Old Man. 'This is a law firm, not a fashion boutique.' He pushed the vase to one side. 'Please continue.'

The Old Man leaned back and shut his eyes. Seyma knew that he was concentrating – she had seen him do the same thing in court. The office manager asked her a few more trivial questions, then ran out of steam.

The Old Man opened his eyes.

'Are you finished?' he asked good-naturedly.

The office manager nodded.

'Excellent. May I ask you a question, Ms. Deled—' The Old Man was unable to pronounce Seyma's surname. 'I'm sorry, would you mind telling me your name again?'

'Deledenkobdülkadir.'

'Delenden—'

'Please, call me Seyma,' she said.

'Thank you. Forgive me,' said the Old Man. 'You know, I don't set much store by people's qualifications, Seyma. Whether a lawyer has what it takes to be a defence lawyer is something you only find out at trial. I know exceptional lawyers who are terrible trial lawyers, and very good defence lawyers who know nothing beyond the Code of

Criminal Procedure. But I read your CV and I was impressed. Qur'an school. Could you tell me a bit about that?'

Seyma looked at the Old Man. The question was an unusual one. She hesitated.

'I went to a Catholic primary school,' she said. 'But from the age of eight I had to attend Qur'an school every weekend – every Saturday and Sunday. It lasted from ten in the morning until six in the evening. My parents insisted I go. The *hoca*—'

'Your religious teacher?' asked the Old Man.

'Yes. The *hoca* said that we would burn in hell if we didn't wear a headscarf. The same went for every other violation of the sacred commandments. As a child, that really scared me.'

'Did the school administer punishments?' asked the Old Man.

'Yes.'

'What were they? And what were they for?'

'Above all, for not paying attention. The teacher would hit our fingertips or knuckles with a stick. It didn't hurt much, but it was humiliating. Which was obviously the idea.'

'What were you taught at the school?' asked the Old Man.

'The Qur'an. According to its teachings, believers are supposed to recite the whole thing at least once in their lives. I recited it five times at the school. The classes were in Turkish, but we read the Qur'an in Arabic.'

'When did you stop going?'

'At seventeen. Although that wasn't the end of it. My father was a miner, but he hired a private tutor, a man who spoke bad Turkish and was constantly sucking boiled sweets.'

'Why?' asked the Old Man.

'My parents wanted me to become a scholar. The *hoca* had suggested it; he thought I was gifted. I was supposed to go to a school for Islamic law. It was viewed as an honour, especially for a girl.'

'And what did you do?' asked the Old Man.

Seyma paused. Then she said: 'I waited.'

'I don't understand,' said the Old Man.

'Every day from the age of twelve, I told myself that I'd be grown-up before too long. The morning after I got my exam results, I finally did what I'd always wanted to do. I threw my headscarf in the bin and haven't worn one since. I phoned the private tutor first thing and told him not to come again. At breakfast I informed my parents that I was going to university. My father was angry. I'd already made it much further than him; I shouldn't push my luck. He wanted me to become a dental assistant because he had great respect for that profession. I like my father very much – he's a brave man and has a big heart. But he's from a different world.'

'And then?' asked the Old Man.

'I moved out, and for a long time I led a double life. To my parents I was still the well-behaved Turkish girl, but of course I lived like every other young woman. My father wouldn't have tolerated me working in clubs, wearing short skirts or having a German boyfriend.' Seyma realised that she'd revealed much more than she had intended. The Old Man looked at her. She held his gaze.

'Why did you choose to study Law?' he asked. His voice was soft. The office manager had already asked her this question and she had answered it. She had talked about the foundations of society, about responsibility, about educational ideals and a love of the law. It had sounded convincing. But now she fell silent.

'Why, Seyma?' he asked again quietly.

'No one can ever be allowed to rule my life again,' she answered just as quietly. 'The law must protect me.'

The Old Man pulled a silver cigarette case from his jacket pocket, snapped it open and then slowly shut it again. The office manager wanted to say something, but the Old Man shook his head.

'If you still want the job, it's yours,' he said. 'Please let us know how much you'd like to be paid and when you can start.'

The Old Man got up and walked over to the door. Then he turned around again.

'Thank you, Seyma, that took a lot of courage,' he said, and left the meeting room.

A week later, Seyma began working at the law firm. For the first four months she read files, made notes and occasionally accompanied lawyers to meetings. Her cases involved fraud, insolvency, breach of trust and insider trading. The files contained thousands of pages of documentation and the lawyers' case papers were hundreds of pages long. The office was professional and well organised, with a courteous atmosphere. The men wore grey or black suits. The women wore outfits in the same colours.

Seyma hardly ever saw the Old Man. He was mostly away; his clients were directors of big companies, bankers, or famous musicians and actors. She'd thought it would be different. This was not the life she wanted.

Every Monday morning at nine, the lawyers met to discuss the firm's current cases. Attendance was compulsory, unless you were in court, off sick or on annual leave. The Old Man seldom took part. But on this particular morning, he and the office manager were in the meeting room long before everyone else.

Seyma sat between her besuited colleagues wearing a long, colourful jumper, with her legs pulled up and her chin resting on her knees. She thought her dark green tights went well with the dark green of the tabletop. She liked those tights because she liked a word on their packaging: 'opaque'.

'We've received instructions from a new client,' said the Old Man. 'The case involves people trafficking, prostitution and related charges. The accused has been on remand for nine months, and the prosecution has been authorised to take the case forward to trial. The previous defence counsel has withdrawn from the case at the request of the accused. I have taken it over. I can't lead on it myself, of course – one of you will have to do that, even though you all have full schedules. The accused is the great-nephew of my very first client.'

The lawyers avoided one another's eyes. By now, Seyma knew that none of them wanted anything to do with cases involving serious criminality. That kind of thing wasn't good for the reputation of the firm, they said. It was distasteful having to represent thieves, pimps and rapists. Corporate criminal law was more of a challenge and the clients were more agreeable.

'So, who would like to deal with this case?' asked the Old Man.

'I'm still tied up with the fiscal proceedings for—' said the oldest of the lawyers working for the firm. He was wearing a very expensive dark blue mohair suit.

'No,' interrupted the Old Man with a smile, 'not anymore. As of this morning, the matter has been unconditionally dropped. Congratulations.'

The man in the mohair suit looked down at the table. Like when you're scared the teacher will pick on you at school, thought Seyma. And in that moment she understood how free she was. The fourteen women and men around the table had very good legal minds and were very good lawyers; they were intelligent and could defend anyone who needed their help. They were liberal, cosmopolitan people. They spoke English, French and Spanish, and one of the younger lawyers, the one with the precise side-parting, even spoke a little Chinese. They kept themselves up to date on political affairs, played golf, went skiing, and had read some of the great literary classics. Their houses and apartments were furnished with Bauhaus lamps, Eames chairs and Le Corbusier chaises longues, and here they discussed vegan school meals, paternity leave and Islamic prayer rooms in kindergartens. They recycled their rubbish and voted for a mainstream political party every four years. But none of them were free and they never would be. That was why the Old Man had hired her. She didn't belong at this table, just as the Old Man hadn't belonged at such tables when he was young and defending terrorists.

'I'd like to take on the case,' she said.

The Old Man looked at her, and nodded. 'It will be difficult and demanding, a psychologically arduous case, a lengthy trial.'

'Even so,' she said.

'Good, then that's settled,' said the Old Man, and smiled.

The discussion moved on, but Seyma was barely listening.

The public prosecutor's office had been investigating the case for three years. The files were almost ten thousand pages long. The charges stated that the client was the head of a gang that transported Ukrainian and Romanian women to Berlin, where it ran a string of brothels. The women were forced into the sex trade.

But it was difficult to prove anything against him. For a long time they didn't have so much as his photograph. The women wouldn't or couldn't give evidence against him. The investigation expanded to four countries. A phone number repeatedly caught the eye of the police, which the authorities believed to be that of the prime suspect.

Two and a half years after the investigation began, a man in a stolen car was arrested by chance following a routine police check. The mobile phone they had been monitoring lay on the passenger seat. The investigators were convinced that this man was their suspect. A warrant was issued to remand him in custody, but even then the police were unable to find any first-hand witnesses. Eventually, the public prosecutor's office was forced to bring charges in order to prevent the man's release. Although the evidence gathered was weak, the court allowed the case to go forward to a full trial.

Seyma accompanied the Old Man on the first visit to see the defendant in custody. Thereafter she was to assume sole responsibility for the case. As they waited in the prison for their client, the Old Man asked her if she was nervous about the trial. No, she said, but that was a lie.

The man wore jeans, a black T-shirt and trainers. Seyma was surprised at how good-looking and friendly he was. He seemed to have a great deal of respect for the Old Man.

The Old Man asked Seyma to summarise the contents of the prosecution case files. She had practised the night before; she wanted to look experienced and professional. After she had completed her presentation and the interpreter had finished translating, the client asked whether that was everything they had against him. Seyma confirmed that it was, and he wanted to know what line of defence she planned to use. He leaned back. She could see some of his tattoos below the hem of his T-shirt. There were photos of his upper torso and legs in the files.

He had a double-headed eagle in garish colours on his chest and a big pair of human eyes on his stomach. The domes of St Basil's Cathedral in Moscow, the Statue of Liberty in New York, US dollar bills and Stalin's head were depicted on his back. There were stars on his shoulders and a naked girl with a fishing rod on his upper right thigh. The tattoos were crudely drawn; he'd had them done while in prison on Sakhalin. The prosecution claimed the tattoos showed he was a senior member of the Russian mafia and a rapist. The Old Man said this wasn't true. The tattoos didn't prove anything, as every Russian prison had its own symbolic imagery, from the Urals to Siberia. Prisoners were tattooed using electric razors, knives or dirty needles, he explained, and many of them contracted tetanus or syphilis as a result. Above all, though, truly important mafia bosses never had tattoos.

Seyma talked the client through the individual pieces of evidence, and explained some minor errors in the investigation and inconsistencies in the files. She said she thought it would be best if he did not speak during the trial. After three hours, the air in the cramped cell was stuffy and everyone felt tired.

As they left the prison the Old Man told her she had done a good job. She should continue to maintain distance between herself and the client, even though that might sometimes be difficult.

'He may not seem it,' said the old lawyer, 'but he's a very dangerous man.'

The trial opened six weeks later. The investigating officers gave evidence for a number of days, documents from Russia and Romania were read out and translated, phone recordings were played to the court. In a gap in the proceedings, the presiding judge said that she was not yet persuaded by the prosecution's case. The client followed Seyma's advice and said nothing.

On the morning of the eighth day, the public prosecutor arrived half an hour late. He was holding a thin sheaf of papers. He said that the police had questioned a new witness late the previous evening. At the moment they had only a short, very cursory statement. The public prosecutor handed the judges and Seyma some photocopied pages.

'The witness was brought here by officials this morning,' he said. 'She's waiting in the corridor. She's frightened and we're concerned she'll go to ground again. I therefore suggest that she be allowed to give evidence today.'

Seyma raised an objection. She needed time to prepare, she said. She had to read the witness statement and discuss the matter with her client.

'With all due respect to the counsel for the defence, it's only two-and-a-half pages,' said the prosecutor.

'How long do you need?' asked the presiding judge.

'At least two days,' said Seyma. 'I'll need to visit my client in custody, and as you know, those meetings always require an interpreter.'

The presiding judge nodded. 'The court needs some time too,' she said. 'On the other hand, we understand the urgency of the public prosecutor's situation. So we'll adjourn until two o'clock and hear from the witness then.' She turned to Seyma. 'Until that time, you may remain here in the courtroom with the defendant and the court interpreter in order to prepare.'

During the adjournment Seyma read her client the witness statement, which was translated for him by the interpreter. The defendant shrugged his shoulders; he had nothing to add.

＊　　＊　　＊

The court reconvened at two o'clock. The young woman sat next to the interpreter on the witness bench in front of the judges. She looked exclusively at the presiding judge. She said that she was not willing to testify with the defendant in the room. She was afraid of him and she was ashamed to speak in front of onlookers. The public prosecutor applied to exclude the defendant and members of the public from the court. Seyma objected again and the presiding judge paused the proceedings.

After a few minutes of consultation the judges returned to the courtroom. The presiding judge said that she would grant the public prosecutor's request. The defendant stood up, smiled and nodded at the witness. A vein throbbed in his neck. Two guards took him back to his cell. The spectators left the courtroom as well.

The witness was hesitant to begin with, but spoke more fluently as time went on. She told the court about her family and about her little sister, who lived with her parents on their farm in a village in Romania. The defendant had promised her that she would make good money as a carer for the elderly in Berlin. Nine hundred euros a month, which was as much as you'd earn back home in a year. She had discussed it with her parents and decided to go. The defendant had been charming and good-looking, and she had been much too young to understand men. As soon as they crossed the border, he had taken away her passport. She wouldn't need it anymore, he'd said.

They had stayed overnight in a barracks on the outskirts of Berlin. It had been dirty, with damp, mouldy walls. Already that first evening he had told her she would have to work for him now; the trip had been expensive, the food and accommodation. She was pretty and could 'work it off'. She had tried to run away, but he'd locked the door.

The next morning she had screamed at him that she wanted to go home. He had stayed perfectly calm and said that in that case, unfortunately, it was time for *subbotnik*. She knew this term from her school-days. *Subbotnik* was a kind of voluntary service, like tidying up the school playground or cleaning the classroom together. But when the defendant used the word *subbotnik* he meant something totally different. He had stood up and opened the door. Five men had entered the room. They looked to her like construction workers; they wore dirty work clothes and stank of sweat. The men had undressed her and tied her to the bed. She had struggled, but hadn't stood a chance.

The men had raped her over and over again. Sometimes they had taken a break and had a few drinks while watching TV. Then they would start up again. They had shoved a beer bottle inside her and urinated on her as well. From what she remembered, it had lasted for hours.

At some point the defendant had come back and sent the men away.

'From now on there'll be *subbotnik* if you don't obey me,' he'd said.

She had told him she would kill herself, but the defendant just laughed.

'I've met your little sister. How old is she? Seven or eight? She's still too young for men. Or maybe she isn't. We'll have to give it a try.' That was what he had said, the words were still etched on her memory. She'd had no other choice but to submit.

The defendant had taken her to a flat in Berlin. She had lived there for two years with six other women and a minder. The other women were in the same situation as her. Every day, she had sex with ten to twelve men. Clients paid 30 euros an hour, and for that they could do what they wanted with her. She saw none of the money and was only allowed to leave the flat once a week with the minder to buy food and cosmetics. She had learned some German from the TV and radio, but never wanted to speak that language again.

Some of the men had demanded things she couldn't bring herself to talk about even now. She wasn't prepared to tell the judge or anyone else what they were. If the women refused to do these things, the defendant would arrive and threaten them with *subbotnik*. Once he had dragged one of the women into his car by her hair. They had all stood at the windows and watched. The woman had never returned.

The young woman gave evidence for a long time. The presiding judge asked about specific details – places, times and names, the type of car the defendant had driven, his phone number. She showed the witness police photos from the case files: of the flat, the room, the street and other suspects. The young woman answered every question.

'How did you escape?' asked the presiding judge.

'I became ill. I lost eighteen kilos and screamed if any man so much as touched me. I simply couldn't bear it any longer. The defendant threatened me with *subbotnik* again, but I didn't even care. I just fell apart. The defendant beat me up. I still wouldn't. He cut my right eye with a knife. Because I was bleeding heavily and they didn't want a body on their hands, the minder taped a plastic bag to my face and drove me to the hospital. He threw me out of the car by the entrance. I'm of no value to men with a face like mine.'

'What happened then?'

'The doctors weren't able to save my eye. The police came and questioned me, but I just kept saying that I'd fallen on some glass. I went back to my family in Romania as soon as I could. That was two years ago.'

'And how have you come to be here in court?'

'Through the Romanian police. Although I never told anyone about Berlin, word got around at home. A couple of weeks ago, two police officers arrived in my village and said they wanted to speak to me. They said that the German authorities had asked them for help. A pimp who'd abducted girls from our area was on trial in Berlin. They were asking women who had been away a long time whether this man had been their pimp. They showed me a photo of the defendant. It was him. Then I spent a while thinking about whether I should testify. In the end, I called the two police officers. They organised everything and I travelled to Berlin with one of them yesterday.'

'And why did you decide to give evidence?' asked the presiding judge.

'Because of the other girls. There are still lots of these flats in the city. I don't know where they are, but that's what I heard a couple of times and I'm sure it's true.'

The presiding judge thanked the witness for giving evidence. She knew what it must have cost her, she said.

'No.' The witness shook her head. 'That's not something you can know.'

Neither the public prosecutor nor Seyma had any further questions. The presiding judge explained that the witness was not required to take an oath, as she was a wronged party. 'Thank you, you may step down now,' said the presiding judge.

The young woman stood up and turned around. Seyma could see her scar, which threaded its way over the right-hand side of her face, from her forehead across her cheek and then down to her chin. Her eye was white. She picked up her handbag and left the courtroom.

The presiding judge asked the guard to fetch the defendant from his cell. She explained to him what the witness had said. It was only much later that everyone realised the mistake she had made.

After the proceedings had finished for the day, Seyma made her way to the S-Bahn station. It was Friday evening. She wished that she were someone else right now, one of the people waiting at the bus stop or reading the newspaper in a café or going home, who knew nothing about the world of the courts. Her apartment felt strange to her. She read her personal emails from the last few months – a dispute with the landlord about a heating bill, a new mobile phone, holiday photos of her friends on the beach. She felt as though someone else had been living her life. She tried to sleep. At three in the morning she got up again and went to a club that had been one of her earlier haunts. People were wearing colourful fluorescent T-shirts, and ultraviolet videos were being projected onto the walls. A young man offered her magic mushrooms from a plastic bag. She bought some and began dancing to the trance music.

The following afternoon she woke up on her balcony in only a T-shirt and couldn't remember how she'd got home.

*   *   *

On Monday, Seyma went to see the presiding judge in her chambers.

'I want to withdraw from the case,' she said.

'As you wish,' said the presiding judge. 'But if you do, I'll assign you to the defendant as his court-appointed defence counsel.'

'You can't do that—' said Seyma.

'I can and I will,' interrupted the presiding judge. 'I won't halt the trial nine days into proceedings just because you'd like to pull out. And I won't ask the witness to give evidence again.'

She gave Seyma an amiable look.

'Is this your first big trial?' she asked.

'Yes,' said Seyma.

'I understand. But that's just how it goes sometimes.'

'I don't want to defend that man any longer.'

'I'm afraid it's not about you. You can't simply withdraw, unless the relationship between you and your client has broken down to such a degree that assigning you as his court-appointed defence counsel is out of the question. That you don't like him or that he doesn't like you isn't reason enough. You've made your aversion to your client plain to me – which could already be viewed a violation of your obligations as a lawyer. But I'll overlook it as it's your first case.'

Seyma was silent.

'I expect you to continue defending your client in a comprehensive and proper fashion,' said the judge. 'That is his and every defendant's right. I'll see you tomorrow in court.'

The defendant was sentenced to fourteen and a half years in prison, six months short of the maximum sentence. On the afternoon of the same day, Seyma lodged an appeal.

It is difficult to bring a successful appeal. The job of the German Federal Court of Justice is not to verify that individuals committed the crime for which they have been convicted. As far as this court is concerned, whether the verdict reflects the truth is immaterial, as long as the trial judge has correctly assessed the evidence. The latter may not be contra-dictory, unclear or incomplete. The length of the sentence is also up to the trial judges, as only they will have had the defendant and the witnesses before them. The trial is not re-enacted for the Federal Court judges, and no witnesses or expert witnesses may be called. Only if the verdict is *legally* flawed – in other words, if a law has been broken – will it be overturned by the Federal Court of Justice. Such instances are rare. The majority of appeals fail.

Seyma was given a written copy of the verdict, after which she had a month to prepare the grounds for appeal. She spent fifteen hours a day in the law firm's library; she avoided others, turned off her phone and ignored her emails. The Old Man regularly looked over what she had written. 'It's not enough,' he would say. 'You need to write more clearly. Your sentences are too complicated. No one will understand what you're trying to say. I don't think you've even fully understood what you're trying to say yourself. You need to keep mulling things over until they become really simple.' He was a tough critic, but she learned a great deal in the course of those days.

In the few hours that Seyma slept, she dreamed about the appeal. After three and a half weeks she found a mistake: the presiding judge had excluded the defendant from the courtroom only for the *duration* of the witness's testimony. That was something she was entitled to do. But then she had released the witness *before* the defendant had returned to the courtroom – and that was wrong. It is the right and the duty of the defendant to be involved in the trial. He is a subject and not merely the object of the criminal proceedings. He is entitled and expected to participate in the decision to release a witness. And that was not something this defendant could do, because he wasn't even present. Of course, the presiding judge hadn't intended to breach his rights. But that was beside the point. The law is strict.

Four months later the Federal Court of Justice overturned the verdict. The trial would have to be held a second time before a different criminal court.

The young woman did not appear as a witness at the retrial. The judges issued a warrant for her. The police were unable to find her, and according to her parents in Romania she had never returned home from Berlin. An anonymous police informant claimed that the woman had been murdered after giving testimony at the first trial and her body dumped, but that couldn't be proved either. A couple of days later, the judges acquitted the defendant. The other evidence had been insufficient to find him guilty.

After the verdict was delivered, Seyma put her laptop and files in her bag and said goodbye to her client.

She spoke briefly to the two reporters who had followed the trial, then went down the steps in the main hall to the exit.

Once outside, she thought about whom she could call, but nobody sprang to mind. She went to a Turkish confectioner in the Kreuzberg district and bought colourful cubes made of sugar, lemon juice, rose water and pistachios, and Turkish baklava. A boy in a white, crisply ironed shirt was standing in the shop. He was looking carefully at the displays that lay behind glass in long rows around three of the walls. He was maybe eight or nine years old. He had just a single coin in his hand and took his time choosing what he wanted. Occasionally he would point at something; the confectioner would say a Turkish word, and the boy would nod happily. Seyma stood by the counter and watched him. She suddenly felt old.

She left the shop, went back to the law firm and found the Old Man. They walked together through the little park, past the fountain and the bench where they had often sat and discussed the trial over the last few weeks. It was bright and warm, a beautiful spring afternoon. They sat at the café in the square, heard the clink of knives and forks, the voices of customers and the shrieks of children in the playground.

'I thought it would be different,' said Seyma.

They ordered coffee, and then they ate the sweets she had bought straight from the bag, until their mouths and tongues were completely sticky.

Tennis

She got back late at night and slept in the guest room so as not to wake her husband. She had just spent a week in Venezuela on a photographic assignment for her employer, a news magazine. Now she stands in the kitchen in front of the open fridge. She stares at her bare feet, which she dislikes, sees the veins under the thin skin. Thinks to herself: *My feet are older than I am.*

She rides her bike down the hill to the club. Her neck looks even more slender than usual in the sun, her thin shoulders sharply defined under the faded T-shirt. She finds the tennis court where he's playing and lets the bike fall onto the grass by the fence. The handlebar has lost its grips and bores into the ground; the earth in it will dry up and fall out again as she cycles. Years ago, he'd wanted to get her a new bike, but she's not very good at parting with things.

*   *   *

She waves to her husband, lies down on the grass and closes her eyes. For a long time she hears only the thwack of tennis balls and the sliding of shoes on the clay court. She had tried it once, back when they had understood one another better, but he had said that tennis wasn't for her; she lacked a feel for the ball. She had felt like an imposition.

She knows that her husband will win. He always wins. He's fifty-seven, she's thirty-six, and they've been married for eleven years. She found the pearl necklace in his bed this morning. She fingers the necklace in the pocket of her trousers; the pearls are smooth and hard. She tries to imagine the other woman. She can't.

After half an hour, she cycles to the lake. In the water she manages not to think about anything. She lies on the warm wood of the jetty, the breeze cool on her skin. When the heat gets too much, she rides back to the house. She's got him some white mountain peaches. They lie in the open bag on the desk.

She turns on her laptop. In an email, the head of the news department asks her to go to Russia, to photograph the 'City Without Drugs' for a piece. He's sorry she has to make another trip so soon, but it's urgent, he writes – her visa has already been arranged. She calls the office. While she's talking on the phone, she plays with the necklace, the beads clacking on the wooden table. She writes her husband a note saying that she needs to get some sleep, but then lies awake all night.

Early the next morning, she stands in the driveway waiting for the taxi. The driver loads her luggage into the boot, and she gets in the back of the car. After ten minutes she asks the driver to turn around. She's forgotten something. The house is dark. She opens the front door quietly. She takes the necklace from her bag and lays it on the top step of the stairs. The pearls gleam on the black granite floor, their exteriors flawless. He'll understand, she thinks, and switches off the light. She only realises at the airport that she's forgotten her phone, but it's too late to go back again now.

In Ekaterinburg, one of the magazine's interpreters picks her up from the airport and drives her to the drug rehab facility. The barracks for the addicts are on the outskirts of the city. It's like being in an old movie about a war hospital. People are lying on bunk beds; it stinks of garlic, sweat and urine. The head of the facility has cropped hair and a bull neck. He says that only a tough approach can help the addicts, otherwise they'd melt down cough sweets containing codeine in spoons and inject the liquid into their veins. Their bodies rot; their skin and bones are eaten away by the phosphorus, iodine and metal; their muscles grow black and hard. They call the drug *krokodil* because it turns their skin scaly. The cough sweets are cheaper than heroin, you can get them everywhere.

She takes photos that she knows are no good. Not far from the interpreter's car, an old man is sitting in the rain, his head between his knees. She fetches the translator and asks the old man why he doesn't go home; it's too cold to be out here and he'll get ill. The rain runs down his face. He doesn't answer at first, but looks up at her from below. Then he says that the *krokodil* ate his daughter. He saw her today: four days after her death he had identified her in the city morgue.

'Why is all this happening?' he asks.

It sounds like a genuine question, and the old man seems to be waiting for an answer as the rain comes down and the water runs inside his collar. She convinces him to go back with her to the hotel. On the way, he leans his forehead against the window. His hair is thin and grey.

At the hotel she has a waiter bring them towels. The old man dries his hair and face, and lays his wet jacket over his knees. He drinks tea and vodka and slowly calms down. The water drips from the chair, turning the carpet dark. The old man says that it's good to talk to someone while drinking hot tea – he hasn't done that for a long time. He tells her about his daughter. Her left leg and right arm had been amputated – the limbs had rotted away – but she'd kept cooking the cough sweets. His son had died in the Chechen War. 'Typhoid,' says the old man. He was eighteen, a boy who hadn't yet loved a girl. Perhaps the daughter couldn't bear it, who knows. They'd never talked about it much.

'We only have this one life,' says the old man, and asks if he can have more tea and more vodka. She wants to give him some money, but the old man won't accept it. 'I'm not a beggar,' he says. He keeps four rabbits in a hutch; they have silky fur and he takes them lettuce every day. He doesn't want money. He needs a person who can explain all this to him in peace. He doesn't understand anything anymore.

Later, she gives him a lift home. The old man's rabbit hutch is on the roof of his block of flats and he wants to show it to her. Although it's still cold, he removes his shirt and picks up one of the rabbits. The rabbit is very warm, he can hear its heart racing – it beats much faster than a human heart, he says. The man's chest hair is grey, like the rabbit's fur and the sky above the houses on that very rainy day.

That night she sleeps deeply and without dreaming. When she wakes, the room is quiet and the air feels stale. She opens the window. Outside, it smells of sulphur from the city's coal stoves. She doesn't have anything from the breakfast buffet. The smell of the coffee makes her feel sick.

The interpreter picks her up and shows her the sights of the city: the cathedrals, the circus, the opera. In a museum shop, she forgets to take her change at the till. When the interpreter asks her questions, she often fails to respond.

* * *

Her flight leaves that evening and she's happy to get on the plane. Just before she falls asleep, she thinks of the holiday they took in the south of France: her husband waiting in the car park by the observation tower while she bought cigarettes for him at the kiosk. He was wearing a white shirt, sleeves half rolled up, his hands in the pockets of his wide trousers. When she returned, he was leaning his body against the wall of the tower, his head tilted back. She had loved him then. She had thought things would work out.

At Frankfurt Airport, her brother is unexpectedly waiting for her. 'Your husband's in hospital,' he tells her. He was unconscious and nobody had been able to reach her in Russia.

~

Three years later she plays in a tennis tournament at her husband's club. She is focused, her strokes hard and precise. She scarcely seems to move at all. She's always in position and hits the balls almost effortlessly. Her tennis instructor says she's a natural.

Later, she sits with her husband on the terrace at home. It was an accident. He hadn't seen the pearls in the dark and had slipped on them. His head had split open on the granite steps of the stairs as he fell: a severe traumatic brain injury. His cerebral cortex functions have been impaired ever since. He can barely speak and is unable to eat independently, or to wash or dress himself.

There's rain forecast this evening; it's getting cooler. She goes in to find him a blanket. In the living room above the sofa hangs the photo of the man with the rabbit. It won an award and made the front cover of the magazine. The late afternoon light falls on the photo through the tall French windows. It shines in an oddly bright way in the semi-darkness of the room. She removes her clothes in front of the picture. Then she goes back out to her husband on the terrace and stands naked before him, her arms behind her back. The only thing she's wearing is the other woman's pearl necklace.

The Friend

Throughout childhood, Richard was my best friend. We'd been sent to boarding school at the age of ten. Our beds were right next to each other, and it was the first time either of us had been away from home. He was the most gifted boy in our year. He got the best marks, played the lead role in school theatre productions, was a striker for the football team, and even won the skiing championships against the locals. Everything seemed to come easily to him and everyone liked being around him. His family lived in Geneva, but his ancestors had helped to found the Ruhr steel industry in the nineteenth century, and his surname featured in our history books.

After his final exams, he read history at Trinity College, Oxford, before spending two years at Harvard Law School. He moved to New York and took a job at the bank that managed his family's assets. A few years later, he got married on a small island off the coast of Thailand; a beach wedding with just a few guests. Sheryl, his wife, was five years younger than him and came from Boston. At the wedding, everyone said she looked like Ali MacGraw, and there was some truth in that.

When his father died, Richard signed over his share of the company to his brother. He and his wife moved into a house in SoHo, Manhattan. They collected artwork, established a charitable foundation and travelled extensively. I visited them once or twice and they were a loving couple. Then contact suddenly broke off and I was no longer able to reach them.

A few years ago, I was involved in an extradition case in New York. My client was embroiled in a string of financial frauds, and both the United States and Germany were keen to bring him to trial. After countless requests and discussions, the American authorities unexpectedly agreed to extradite him to Berlin, and I had a free day in New York. I called Richard's brother in Geneva. He said that Richard had been living in a hotel for the past four years; perhaps I could visit him there.

I went to the address and an elevator boy took me up to the forty-second floor. I rang the bell and waited a long time. It was an expensive hotel with marble floors and thick carpet runners. The hallway smelled of cleaning products, and mirrors and gold-framed architectural drawings of the old building hung on the walls.

A young woman opened the door. Her eyes were puffy and she was wearing just a T-shirt. She left the door standing open and went into the bedroom without a word. Richard lay on a sofa. His shirt was hanging open and one side was ripped. I had never seen such a thin man. When he saw me, he sat up. Like a child, without saying hello, he started telling me all about the TV series he was watching. A mass of colourful tablets wrapped in cellophane were lying on the table.

'It was a long night,' he said. His eyes were glassy.

He stood up and hugged me. He smelled of sweat and alcohol. The corners of his mouth were cracked, his skin was scaly and dry, there was encrusted blood beneath his nose. His head was bloated and seemed too large for him.

'We're going out,' he said. It took him ages to find his sunglasses.

It was muggy down on the street. A homeless man was washing his face in water from a fire hydrant.

There was the usual city soundscape: the roar of cars, staccato honking, police and ambulance sirens. We walked up East 63rd Street. Richard kept stumbling. 'The only diner around here with decent coffee is on the corner of Madison,' he said.

We took seats in a booth and waited. Everyone seemed to know him here. A driver from Rockwell's Bakery delivered sliced bread for toasting and stacked it in the compartments over the counter. The boss of the diner gave his cook a kick up the backside for being too slow, and the customers laughed and applauded. The boss took a bow; the cook grinned. A waiter brought us two takeaway paper cups. The coffee was hot and strong. We walked back, crossed Fifth Avenue and sat in a meadow in Central Park. Richard's hands trembled, the coffee ran down his three-day stubble, and when he tried to wipe it off, he ended up pouring the rest of the cup down his shirt. Girls in yellow East Harlem T-shirts were warming up for a baseball game, and shrieking like schoolchildren all over the world. We watched them.

'It happened there,' said Richard suddenly, pointing at the path.

'What do you mean?' I asked.

He didn't answer. He lay back on the grass and immediately fell asleep. His mouth fell open, his face looked pale and sweaty.

Later, I woke him and took him back to the hotel. The young woman was gone. I told him that if he wanted to survive, he'd have to go into rehab – the drugs would kill him. He let himself fall onto the sofa, knocking over a lamp in the process, and tried to right it again twice before giving up. It's not that bad, he said, and turned the TV back on. All addicts lie.

Before leaving, I spoke to the hotel manager. I gave him some money, asked him to check on Richard regularly, and left him the brother's phone number. I thought that was all I could do.

Two years later Richard sent me an email. He was in France now, he said – could I pay him a visit? I knew the house in Normandy, I'd often been there as a child. Back then, Richard's mother always used to sit in the garden with a book – a quiet, slim woman with dark eyes, who wore a black cardigan even at the height of summer. I only found out later that she had spent most of her life in a psychiatric clinic. It was in her garden above the sea that I saw orange and lemon trees for the first time.

I parked the car by the fountain and walked past the house down to the garden. Richard was sitting in the little gazebo in a wicker chair, a plaid blanket over his knees. On the table next to him were tea things, pastries and a vase of quince branches. A bronze angel, weathered and oxide-green, stood next to the gazebo. As children we had shot at it with arrows.

Richard's face was still sunken, the skin stretched over the cheekbones. His hair was now cropped short; he wore a cap made of thick tweed.

'So good that you could come,' he said. 'You're the first visitor I've had in months.'

His speech was no longer slurred; his eyes looked clear and simultaneously very tired. His coat seemed to be a couple of sizes too big for him.

'Did you meet the Dragon?' he asked.

'The Dragon?'

'The nurse. She's awfully strict. My brother chose her.'

We talked about childhood times at the house. I reminisced about the gardener who'd had only one tooth, our illicit excursions to the village, and the priest's pretty daughter, who had fallen in love with Richard. All of our memories are profane and all of them are sacred.

'They want me to see a therapist,' he said suddenly.

'And will you?'

'No,' he said. 'There's nothing to treat. I was at a clinic in Geneva and everyone had a go. I'm not doing it again. Talking doesn't help.'

The sea was grey. It would rain that night, the kind of soft drizzle that only fell here.

'Do you still smoke?' he asked. 'The Dragon's forbidden it, but I really need a smoke right now.'

I gave him a cigarette. He lit it, took a drag, and immediately started to cough. He laughed and stubbed it out on a saucer.

'Can't even do that anymore,' he said.

'I should quit too,' I said, simply to have something to say.

Richard put his feet up on another chair and rested his teacup on his stomach.

'I haven't been to the village in ages. My brother had the church renovated and I'd like to see it. But I can't, the Dragon's forbidden that as well. It feels just like the old days: 'Stay in the garden!'

We laughed. Then we drank our tea, which had gone cold. For a long time, we said nothing.

'What happened?' I finally asked.

'Do you remember old Tack-Tack?' said Richard.

'Of course.' At boarding school, we had called our German teacher Tack-Tack because of his speech impediment. A Jesuit priest who had adored Rilke.

'Remember that poem? "Who speaks of winning? Survival is all".'

'We had to learn it off by heart.'

'Rilke was thinking about the war then,' said Richard. 'I'm not sure he really believed what he wrote. In any case, I now know that it's nonsense. Survival means nothing. Absolutely nothing.'

The scent of roses, tulips and lilies of the valley had grown very strong.

'You know,' he said, 'I really loved Sheryl. It may not have been what they call a great love exactly, but we got along really well, better than most couples we knew. Then we tried to have a baby. It didn't work. We joked about it to begin with. But Sheryl took it more and more seriously. She scheduled the times we had to have sex according to her basal body temperature. It all got horribly embarrassing. We consulted doctors, tried everything; my sperm was tested, I gave up smoking. Each time she got her period, it was a fresh defeat. The setbacks became harder to deal with from month to month. From the outside, it must sound stupid; after all, we had nothing else to complain about in our lives. But she became more and more desperate, she cried and cried. We no longer went anywhere: no trips, no concerts, no exhibitions. We ate only at home. Our lives became small and ugly. Sheryl didn't want any visitors. She even fired our housekeeper – *I can't stand that woman any longer*, she said. And she said the same of all of our friends at some point. When I saw other couples on the street, I envied their lightness. I was jealous of people just because they kissed or went to the cinema together. In the evenings, I watched travel documentaries on TV. Can you imagine? Me watching idiotic travel and animal documentaries.'

'I know what you mean,' I said.

'There was a small room in our house that overlooked the communal courtyard at the back. We called it the office, but it actually just had my computer in it and an armchair with a lamp. Every day, a little boy was out in the courtyard. He had a cat. Hour after hour he knelt on the hot concrete and stroked her. I don't know how long I watched him do it. I wanted my life back, do you see? I couldn't leave Sheryl. We'd been through so much together and she was suffering just as badly as me. I was too much of a coward to tell her we had to stop trying. Out of fear and guilt and stupidity, I went along with the madness. And then at some point, that long, hot summer was over. We were ground down and tired, and suddenly it wasn't working anymore.'

'What did you do?'

'I told her. I promised her I'd be there for her, but that I just couldn't do it anymore. I wasn't the man she needed. We stood in the kitchen in front of the dinner she had cooked. We didn't argue or raise our voices, we never did that – it wasn't our style. Sheryl said that she understood, and then she started to cry, that terrible silent crying. She went into the bedroom and put on her jogging gear. Whenever she wanted to think, she'd ride her bike all the way up to Central Park and run for an hour.'

Richard took another cigarette, started coughing again, but this time he kept smoking.

'When they found her,' he said, 'her skull was shattered. She had lost eighty per cent of her blood. They found twigs, leaves and earth in her vagina. It was two men, eighteen and twenty years old. They took her mobile, necklace and wedding ring. They probably didn't mean to kill Sheryl. It was more of an accident, I think. They were later convicted of murder.'

'I had no idea,' I said.

'Sheryl had kept her maiden name. The newspapers reported the case anonymously, and my brother managed to keep the press away. I'm not sure how, but he's very skilled at these things. I stuck it out for a few more weeks at our place. You know – funeral, formalities, condolence visits, the whole works. But then I had to get myself out of that prison and out of my head, where I was constantly on my own. I moved into the hotel and began to destroy myself. I did it consciously and systematically. You know the rest.'

'Did you go to the trial?'

'No. I didn't want to be in the same room as those men. I got the files from the lawyers, the photos too. They're upstairs in the safe.'

Richard stopped talking. I heard him breathing, but I couldn't look at him.

'*You're so far away*. That was the last thing she said to me. I watched from the kitchen window as she unlocked her bike and cycled off up the street.'

'You mustn't feel guilty,' I said.

'Yes, that's what everyone says. They think those sorts of phrases will help. But if I had held her in my arms, if I had said we'll do things differently now, or if I had just taken her away, then she would still be alive. It *is* my fault and nothing can change that. No therapy and no amount of drugs. She's gone and she's still here, and I can't bear both at the same time.'

He stood up and walked to the edge of the cliff. I joined him. Together, we looked at the waves crashing against the rocks below.

'Perhaps you're right, and there's no crime and no guilt,' he said. 'But there is a punishment.'

When I left two hours later, my friend was still sitting in the gazebo: wrapped up, motionless, silent. It was the last time I saw him. Two weeks later he dissolved a few grams of pentobarbital sodium in a tooth mug and swallowed it. No one could say how he had got hold of the drug. He was buried in New York next to his wife.

A few months after that day in Normandy I started writing. It had all become too much. Most people have never encountered violent death. They don't know what it looks like, how it smells, or about the emptiness it leaves behind. I thought of all the people I had defended, of their loneliness, their otherness, and the horror they felt about themselves.

After my twenty years as a criminal defence lawyer, all that remained was a cardboard box. Bits and pieces:

a green fountain pen that no longer wrote very well, a cigarette case that a client had given me, a few photographs and letters. I thought a new life would be easier, but it never did get easier. It's just the same, whether we're pharmacists or carpenters or writers. The rules are always a little different, but the otherness remains, and so does the loneliness and everything else.